PRAISE FOR The Fly Fish'd and Lies of Suffering

Peyton Burgess is an original—a gifted, entertaining, unprecedented original. These stories have style, heart, brains and a sense of humor, and I can't imagine a reader who wouldn't want to put this at the heart of the bookshelf. Just read it.

—**Darin Strauss**, National Book Award winning author of *Half a Life*

In these stories of physical and emotional dislocation, Peyton Burgess brings us one wonderfully blighted hero after another—hapless but not hopeless, pummeled by the ills of our society but lucid and funny and soldiering on. Burgess is a profoundly gifted writer who understands that for art to exist, there must be scars.

—**Elizabeth McKenzie**, author of *The Portable Veblen*

These stories will leave you in fits of laughter just as often as they'll break your heart. They'll seduce you, trick you, and leave you bewildered that you're just now discovering a talent like Burgess.

—**Grant Ginder**, author of *People We Hate at the Wedding*

Do people really want to be saved? Or do we love our lack? As we look for mothering in line at the post office or cook something humble with name brand equipment, are we preoccupied with re-shaping absence, battering and frying it over and over till insufficiency becomes the comfort food of our being? Our storyteller in *The Fry Pans Aren't Sufficing* thinks: "Mostly, I'm beginning to question my value." Indeed, the very deepest core of value is investigated in the midst of natural disaster, unfathomable personal loss, and systemic injustice in this collection of experientially accessible yet existentially confrontational stories. Burgess' casually sensual language and visceral relatability make lack all the more felt.

—**Monica McClure**, author of *Tender Data*

The Fry Pans Aren't Sufficing is funny, but this collection also divines an elemental loneliness. I know these people, their voices, their lives caught between earthy double-entendres in the fun-loving Crescent City. The hard-edged comedy of Burgess's narrative is shaped and honed, always merciful, and is peppered with dialogue that's reliable and masterfully executed. Personal and surreal, these poignant survival stories coax the reader into moments of shared feeling, into truth, reflection, and simple beauty.

—**Yusef Komunyakaa,** Pulitzer Prize winning author of *The Emperor of Water Clocks* and *The Chameleon Couch*

THE FRY PANS AREN'T SUFFICING

PEYTON BURGESS

Lavender Ink
New Orleans
lavenderink.org
∿

The Fry Pans Aren't Sufficing
by Peyton Burgess
Copyright © 2016 by Peyton Burgess and Lavender Ink
All rites reserved. No part of this work may be reproduced etc.

Printed in the U.S.A.
First Printing
10 9 8 7 6 5 4 3 2 1   16 17 18 19 20 21

Cover art: Bianca Stone
Cover design: Benito Segovia
Book design: Bill Lavender

Library of Congress Control Number: 2016935531
Burgess, Peyton
The Fry Pans Aren't Sufficing / Peyton Burgess
p. cm.

ISBN: 978-1-944884-01-7 (pbk.)
978-1-944884-02-4 (ebook)

Lavender Ink
New Orleans

CONTENTS

ONE

TWO

THREE

THE FRY PANS AREN'T SUFFICING

For my parents, and for Ryan

ONE

THE FRY PANS AREN'T SUFFICING

Normally I don't go to USPS mail recovery auctions. I didn't even know they existed. But they exist once a month at the Mail Recovery Center in Atlanta. This month, September, and this day, the 29th, it's an all day event.

I'd gone to the post office to mail FEMA the claims for my Camry and my apartment. Also, it'd seemed like a good excuse to get out of Baby Girl's mom's house and find a way to not go back immediately because my routine there alone all day, while everybody else is at work or school, has become what must be unhealthy. I have two rum and cokes by noon. Since evacuating to Atlanta, my biggest accomplishment each day amounts to cooking dinner for everyone and making sure that there's a vegetarian option for the little sister. When I'm at their house alone all day, their yellow and grey cockatiel chirps incessantly. Once Chico sees that I've gotten up to drink coffee he'll follow me to the bathroom and wait outside the door and I can't shit with him tapping around on the hardwood floors. I don't like touching Chico because the thought of his dander is the fact something awful, so I never place him in his cage. Also, Baby Girl likes the idea of him roaming free in the house. It isn't until noon, shortly after the rum and cokes, when I can pick up Chico and put him in his cage. Mostly I'm beginning to question my value.

So here at the mail auction: I think of Chico to keep myself from just retreating back home. I'm hanging around the fluorescent-light-induced fuzz of the mail recovery center; I'm interested enough to watch how the government rids itself of unclaimed mail etc. The large room has that same low-ceilinged expansive quality that I recall from public school cafeterias, and it makes me just as unsure of where I will sit as it did in the sixth grade. But this is just the kind of pressure I need lately: a healthy, doable challenge. I can imagine somebody telling me that.

Postal employee Dara Walsh is filing bidder forms, using her long, painted fake nails to separate the sheets of paper. Her nails are painted with these intricate designs but I can't make out the designs. She's explaining to a coworker why she was late. Something about the school bus never showing up on time and she didn't want to leave little man alone at the bus stop. Andy, whom I assume is Mr. Walsh, was still at his night shift for AT&T because they're doing a big digital install, and Dara doesn't trust the other parents or their kids because East Point can be rough sometimes. When she really wants to make her point, like emphasize something especially, she stops filing and raps her nails against the table. All of this makes me love Dara immediately and I feel like I could tell her anything. She's luminous. Her skin is café au lait and her forearms are beignets and I'd say she's a good fifty. She hasn't made eye contact with me yet so I continue reading over the fine print on the back of the bidder form but mostly I'm just listening to Dara because now she's talking about this place in Decatur that has good burgers. I can appreciate a good burger. It's the kind of burger that's cooked in its own fat on a griddle that both Dara and I prefer. I really love Dara.

She has the same manner I enjoyed in the ladies at courthouses I visited for work back home—this nurturing sweetness that's in her smile and comes with her unwillingness to pay attention to me. I hope she calls me her "little cracker baby." Weird, I know, but that's how it always was. I have this ugly, pull-hair-inducing desire to be mentioned in her obituary.

Dara calls me "young man" and asks if I need anything. "You look lost," she says, smiling and then laughing with her coworker. "If you're looking to mail something, go around that corner and take your next right."

I do look lost. Most of the people attending the Mail Recovery Center's September 29ᵗʰ unclaimed mail auction are probably the exact same people that attend all the other unclaimed mail auctions throughout the year. They talk to each other with the kind of familiarity you see at the conclusion of a Baptist worship. I imagine they go in big groups to Denny's. They ask the servers to push the tables together.

I hope Dara looks at me and thinks to herself that I need help. I want her to ask me what the Allstate adjuster said when he called me. He had called a couple days ago and said my car was definitely totaled. "Definitely?" I asked. "Yes, sir. Like God sneezed all over the inside. Goop. That's the only way I can describe it," he answered with what I will call a Texan accent. But a car is just a car. I'll get over it.

Although I love Dara and I really do get the feeling that I could tell her anything, even everything, I'm professional.

"Dara, how does this work?" I ask her.

"You've been reading that form for ten minutes now. What else is to know?"

"Do they know exactly what they're bidding on?"

"Well, they're not gonna bid on the boxes. They bid on what's inside the boxes. See when the police officer gets here we'll start the inspection and open them up. The officer is here in case there's any contraband. Like weed or something."

I'm surprised by how suddenly I decide to steal the contraband. I don't even smoke weed that much, but if there's a shitload of weed in one of those boxes I'm going to take it. It would end up improving things somehow.

I've been told that I'm really good at accomplishing things. I can hear somebody saying it right now: *You can steal those drugs because you said you're going to steal those drugs so do it, man.*

I hear that in my head, and then I realize nobody I know talks like that.

The cop walks in with what sounds like ninety keys jingling from his belt. The sounds immediately make me aware of his size and power, which somehow are endless because even though he stops walking I swear the sounds of his keys jingling still echo through the room.

"Morning, Will," says Dara.

Will, the cop, doesn't say anything. But he lets out a huff as he crashes down into a plastic chair. He is a large man. Will leans forward and puts his forearms on the table, which moans with his weight. His forearms are like my thighs, but my thighs are like the complexion of tracing paper and his forearms are a dark black like volcanic soil, other than that there's no difference between this cop's forearms and my thighs. I think about how hard those forearms could swing his club against my slightly small frame. I'm not that small, 5-9, 170 pounds. But Will is like 6-4. *You're so determined. You can accomplish anything. You really can. You can steal those drugs because you said you're going to steal those drugs so do it, man.* I hear that in my head and I realize nobody talks like that because nobody wants to watch anybody get beat up by Will, right?

I stay anyway.

"Really? You're staying?" says Dara. "I don't mean to sound rude, but you don't seem like the type that would be here." Dara taps all ten of her intricately painted nails on the table to indicate "here."

It's suddenly all in front of me. Dara has the Atlanta skyline painted across her nails. I've heard of it, but I've never actually seen it. Is there a special stencil or something? I can't imagine somebody doing that freehand every time a customer asks for the skyline.

"It's okay, Dara. I don't take offense. I like you. I guess this just looks interesting."

"It's not."

"Okay. So that's the Atlanta skyline on your nails?"

"Some of it."

I fill out the bidder's form because I'm sick of cooking dinner for Baby Girl's family without a decent skillet or a Dutch oven. The fry pans aren't sufficing. So maybe I could luck out and get some Le Creuset on the cheap. But I really can't afford to get into a bidding war with any of these people, these hoarders. And the problem with hoarders, I'm going to observe imperfectly, is that even if all of them have a Creuset signature 11-piece cookware set, there are at least seven different colors to choose from and for hoarders to be satisfied they would need an 11-piece set in all seven colors, including Dune, Lemongrass, and Cassis.

Dara hands me a black bidder's paddle with the number 63 marked in white.

"Good luck, Honey. Hope you at least have some fun."

I take the last seat in the back, by a woman holding a bidder's paddle with the number 52. Bidder's paddle feels like the right phrasing but I'm not sure what they're actually called. It's safe to assume that if I refer to the bidder's paddle thing as a bidder's paddle then everybody would know exactly what I'm talking about. This kind of improvisation helps me adapt to my new world since evacuating. Hero sandwich thing = po'boy, EZpass remote toll payer thing = 50 cents, couch futon fold-out thing = bed, standing-up through boxer shorts and lifted nightgown hungry muffled sex thing = not lovemaking, bidder's paddle thing =

Something like that. I haven't figured it out all the way. I guess all the improvised words are sort of long and exhausting because things got complicated and hard to clearly define. Sex doesn't happen because we can't be sleeping in the same bed at her mom's house because we're young and not married and they're all Catholic and I don't want to be disrespectful. It just seems impossible to schedule horniness and privacy concurrently. But sometimes Baby Girl and I accidentally do it when we say goodnight to each other, thus standing-up through boxer shorts and lifted nightgown hungry muffled sex. It's not so bad because it's hungry and slightly impulsive still. But it's gotten less and less frequent; in fact, I don't remember the last time it happened. Baby Girl and I had been discussing the possibility of adding fierce to the improvised word, maybe in between hungry and muffled. Now though, the elements of fierce and hungry are gone. We both think things have gotten stupid enough that we might as well make it more complicated. It's a kind of giving up. And now we both have our own perfect excuses to start over.

Bidder's paddle number 52 sits with her ankles crossed and her hands clasped calmly around her bidder's paddle on her lap. It's going to make more sense, or it will just be easier, if I just refer to her as 52 from now on.

52 sits with her ankles crossed and is scratching the side of her head with her bidder's paddle. 52's red hair treatment is in need of a touch-up but her aqua nails look great. She's maybe 65 years old. She keeps scratching her head though, so I wonder if the hair treatment is causing some damage to her scalp. "How are you?" I ask.

"Just another day," 52 says.

"It's funny you say that because I'm sort of on an adventure today," I say, waving my bidder's paddle as if to say hello to her.

"Right now?" she asks.

"Yeah." I immediately feel defeated and express it by staring at my feet like a child.

"Hey I'm sorry," 52 says. "You know, it's the second time this week my son, my only offspring, cancelled lunch on me. So I came here because that's what I normally do, except for when my son takes me out to lunch."

"I understand."

"Do you?"

"Not entirely."

"Sometimes I'm embarrassed to be here." 52 covers her face with her bidder's paddle. "I think Dara feels sorry for me," she mumbles against the paddle.

I can see Dara feeling sorry for her. Dara does come across as a sympathetic person. I think Dara was starting to feel sorry for *me*. Maybe that's what we all want from Dara. That's unfair to her.

"Yeah. I really love Dara," I say.

"She's a nice lady."

"I'm Gil, but you can call me 63."

52 and I shake hands.

"Okay, 63," she laughs. "You can call me Patty."

Patty and I look to the front as Will the cop starts digging through boxes with his my-thighs-sized forearms. He's wearing some thick-looking green rubber gloves that don't crease or fold very much, even on his big hands.

The first item no shit is a Le Creuset skillet just like mine, except in Lemongrass. The bidding starts at $70. I don't bid but my chair is tilting forward as I try to get a good look at who *is* bidding. I'm feeling oddly competitive. And there's something reaffirming about that. A man, he's bald, sitting in the front row, immediately bids $120. He wins it without a challenge from anybody else.

The next item again is a Le Creuset skillet, except in Dune. The bidding starts at $60 and again the bald man up front wins without a challenge, offering $110 this time.

Will the cop blows my mind as he pulls out another Le Creuset skillet. He holds it up high in the air like a new father showing off his baby to the townsfolk or something. It's Cherry, the color. It's the same exact 11 ¾ inch skillet I have back home. No joke. It's a cherry red skillet.

"I got to have that skillet. That's *my* skillet," I say, my knees bent a little like I'm afraid to stand up.

"The Le Creuset?" 52 asks.

"Yes. The Le Creuset." I laugh a little bit. "I have one just like it back home."

"Then what do you want another one for?" 52 adjusts herself in her chair as if she's actually bothered.

"I don't know if I have it anymore. It could be rusted or soaking in sewage or something. You know. Like God sneezed. Goop!"

"Why on earth? What are you talking about, Gil?"

"It's hard to explain."

"I doubt it is. Either you have the skillet or you don't. And I don't mean to burn your grits but Harold, number 33 there, is hard to beat when it comes to high-end, unclaimed mail." 52 points to the bald man sitting up front, in the middle.

I stand up to get a better look at 33. He's sort of hunched, slouching over his prized Le Creusets and what looks like a notepad.

"He does all his Christmas and birthday shopping here for his family. I think he has a big family. He drives an Econoline."

"An Econoline?"

"It's a conversion van. It probably seats twelve." 52 says this sadly. And I think of her only offspring canceling lunch on her. And I want to tell Patty it's okay.

"He's an asshole, Patty."

"Anyway, Gil, I just don't want you to get too excited. He's a tough bidder. He's got the money, compared to us anyway."

I guess it's fair for Patty to make assumptions about my financial limitations. I haven't been able to rebuild my wardrobe yet, depending on one pair of jeans and a Red Hot Chili Peppers t-shirt. The Chili Peppers aren't even a go-to band for me. I haven't figured out an improvised word to describe the general situation. I imagine it's so long that it's not even worth saying.

The Le Creuset 11 ¾ inch cast iron skillet is covered in enamel that is pretty accurately painted the color of a cherry. It's got shades that go from bright red to like a red-finished wood tinge. That transition is important. I'd paid $125 for the skillet because I had a good job.

I think I can do $50 for this one right now.

"Patty, I can go up to $50."

"Gil, that's a lot of money for a skillet. Ace has one for $20. It's not pretty and red but it's good."

"I know. But that one is special." My thoughts earlier about hoarders and how they want more than one of one thing really make it weird for me to say that. But what does Patty know?

Will the cop holds my Le Creuset skillet in the air, the Cherry red glowing white under the fluorescent lights. He starts the bidding at $50.

I hold my bidder's paddle with my number 63 as high as I can. My heart backfires and throws some nausea in my throat. If I was ever an athlete I imagine that this is how it would feel throwing the winning shot at the basket right as the clock comes to its zeros.

I steady myself on Patty's shoulder as I reach higher into the air with my bidder's paddle thing. I feel her hand pat mine reassuringly, or sympathetically. The bidding price immediately goes up to $90. It goes up so fast I'm not able to make a bid. It sells to 33.

"He is a fucking asshole, Patty." I sit back down, throwing my bidder's paddle on the ground. I never want to see a bidder's paddle again or even say the words. Ever again. It makes me sick. At this point. Just thinking of those words.

"Come on, Gil. Are you hungry? I'll get you a Whopper next door."

I hate Whoppers. But Patty is really nice and she knows everything. She's there for me. She saw this coming. I'd like a chocolate milkshake.

Dara is tapping her long Atlanta skyline nails on the table, looking bored.

"I love you, Dara," I say to Dara as Patty and I leave.

"Oh honey, you can't win everything at this show."

Patty and I lean against the trunk of her blue Taurus and she eats a Whopper and I try to suck down my chocolate milkshake. I give up and take the top off, and end up just getting it all over my nose and upper lip.

Patty talks about her husband and their old house on Long Island and how she moved to Atlanta to be near her son after her husband died.

I tell Patty that Baby Girl and I will probably be moving back home any day now. And that it's no big deal that I didn't get that Le Creuset today because I'm sure mine is right on the stove where I left it. "Just needs to be cleaned with hot water and oil," I say.

I'm reminded of a woman who once wrote something about Southerners being cynics disguised as romantics and Northerners being romantics disguised as cynics and I'm still not sure.

"Here," Patty says. She turns around and fiddles through her purse for her keys. "Move your butt."

I slide off her car. She opens her trunk and pulls out a box. It's a Cuisinart Elite 14-Cup Food Processor.

"It's brand new. Never opened. I got it at the mail auction last month. I was going to give it to my son today, but he won't be missing it," she says.

I take the Cuisinart and I open Patty's door for her and she collapses down onto the seat in a clumsy way that makes me worried for her. She grabs the door and shuts it herself as she turns the ignition. I pat the Cuisinart Elite and she waves me off. I walk to the bus stop trying to cram the Cuisinart under my arm.

When I get back to Baby Girl's mom's house I put on a mix CD of Louis Prima and Tom Zé, which is a weird mix but I like to keep it real. I pull out vegetables and boil the thin spaghetti. The Cuisinart Food Processor chops zucchini, onions, red peppers, yellow peppers, green peppers, orange peppers, and garlic just like I would, except all at the same time, so faster. Baby Girl comes through the door and she kisses me on the cheek. She stretches, she swings a leg behind her to pop her hip, and then the other. She jumps up to sit on the counter and gets chopped onion all over herself. Her dark blonde hair is greasy and stuck to her head from running her hands through it each time she would sit back from her computer at her new temp gig. I dump the veggies in a kind of crappy stir fry pan. She hooks my waist with her foot and then wraps her legs around me, squeezing me tight. We kiss more. The vegetables pop in the oil and her little sisters and mom come through the door. They're fighting about the proper speed for going over a speed bump. We stop kissing, but she keeps her legs around me and tugs me back to her when I try to pull away. Her sisters continue arguing and her mom checks the voicemail because she knows I never answer their phone. Baby Girl pulls me close enough that I can smell a weirdly erotic mixture of chocolate, croissant pastry, and honey skin lotion on her neck.

"Do you want to go out for dinner? Just the two of us," Baby Girl says.

"No," I say.

She lets me loose from her legs. And she frowns.

ON THE WAY END

We'd decided to spend my birthday driving home.

It's Thursday, so if everything's somehow back to normal somebody will be grilling something around ten that night on until four in the morning.

"Thibodeaux!" I'm yelling into my phone. The wind is blowing loud through our car windows. "Hey, Thibodeaux. We're in Hattiesburg."

"Yeah? I'm at Molly's!" he yells, music scratching through from the background so I can barely understand him. He yells something else I don't understand.

I get the point and hang up my cell. We have just two hours left in the drive.

"Just enough time to make something. Somebody's gotta be playing something," Baby Girl says. She's rubbing the edge of her pencil against the car's vinyl dash. She raises the pencil and peers at the tip with one eye and then blows the dust off it as she goes back to sharpening it against the dash's rough vinyl.

Besides it being my birthday, it would also be our first night back home since we'd evacuated to Baby Girl's mom's house in Atlanta. We had rolled out of the 285 perimeter with that sounternplayalisticadillacfunkymusic busting from the trunk, nervous to see home but excited to hear a horn swooning through open windows and riding on humidity. I'd purchased a 1994 Jetta with the $2,000 car insurance payout from my Camry. I wasn't picky about the Jetta. It just needed to get me five hundred miles south.

I had been bad in Atlanta. Complained about the crummy food, the janky fry pans, no privacy, no sex. We were guests everywhere. I whined a few times about taking Mass too and then just stopped going. The whole thing had been a serious drag on both of us and whatever Baby Girl and I had going wasn't going anywhere anymore. We hadn't said it to one another, but it was clear that once we got back we'd use the chaos and the adventure to go our separate ways, disappear, and start anew, as they say.

The Jetta looks pretty good. It has an amplifier and an eight-inch woofer that sometimes works.

"Something's burning," Baby Girl says, cranking her window down a bit more.

"Yeah. Like burning plastic," I say and look at the engine's temperature gauge, exhausting the extent of what I know about cars.

"Look." She shows me the charcoal drawing she's been doing on her big sketchpad. It's a giant drawing of Baby Girl giving some trumpet blower a big hug. She's copying it from a photo that's taped over the right A/C vent so she can look at it while she draws. All you can see in the drawing though is her smile and the dude's cheeks blowing up on his horn. I try not to think too much of it.

"That's encouraging," I say.

"Relax," she says.

The four-cylinder screams a buzz as I top off fifth gear, a fly on the scent of the rot that awaits us. I'm high on the cash that sits in my account, more loaded than I've ever been, $6,000 in the bank from a FEMA check I got for my flooded cottage. Baby Girl has even more, maybe $8,000. We would spend it on beer and food at the restaurants that had managed to open, new linens, clothes. We'd go to the dentist at one of those non-profit medical encampments and get our teeth cleaned. That'd be a step in the right direction. Then I'd wait for Baby Girl to ditch me, and I'd move my butt Uptown or Mid I guess.

But that smell Baby Girl picked up on quickly turns into

smoke. Then little blue flames lurch out of the steering column and lick at my lap and Baby Girl's bare brown legs. Baby Girl hugs the big sketchpad against her chest and pulls her legs up onto the seat, yelling, "Pull over! Goddamn, it's coming out the A/C!"

I stomp down on the brakes and clutch and screech the Jetta to a stop in the emergency lane. Baby Girl snatches the photo off the dashboard. After grabbing some clothes from the backseat, we slam the doors and watch the fire quickly spread through the cloth interior. We run about thirty yards back north thinking the car's going to blow up. Will we have to dive over the hedges for cover?

The flames fill the inside of the car quickly but then grow at an agonizingly boring sputter.

"Why doesn't it just explode?" Baby Girl says.

"Yeah, this is nothing like the movies," I say.

The windows crack and shatter in slow volley, making sounds like the first corn kernels popping in a microwave. More oxygen whips at the fire. The flames grow and soon engulf the whole car, reaching twelve feet high. The gasoline from our full tank slowly trickles more fire onto the pavement. But the car refuses to explode.

Baby Girl lets out a whimper. "What the hell, man?" Her shoulders slump and she lets her sketchpad drop to the ground.

That bothers me. Baby Girl never cries, or she cries rarely enough that I'm not sure when she last cried. I don't remember seeing her cry ever. Maybe I just figured out a way to ignore it.

"It's okay. It's just a car. I only had the thing for three days anyway so who cares," I say as we stand on the side of the road.

In what I realize is a selfish attempt to distract her from her own fears, I say, "This is one shitty birthday I'm having."

So she wipes her face dry. "Don't worry. We'll get home tonight," she says.

We watch the car burn from our shadowy safe place on the side of I-59, and we start seeing red lights flash against the wall of storm-splintered pine trees. Suddenly a police cruiser comes tearing across the median, slamming its brakes and screeching as it slides to a stop by our burning car. The cop jumps out and runs up to our automotive bonfire, shielding his eyes from the heat as he tries to look for survivors.

"Is anybody in there? Oh, Lord, please!" the cop yells.

"Oh shit," I laugh.

"Hey, hey!" Baby Girl starts jumping up and down. "We're over here! We're right here!" She turns and looks at me. "It's not funny. He's freaking out."

She picks up her sketchpad and runs toward the cop, waving and yelling, holding that giant sketchpad up like some kind of flag, the back of her long-limbed body black against the light of the fire. She reaches the cop and he stumbles back in alarm and then he grabs her shoulders in relief. He looks at me. By now the flames are big enough that I can feel the warmth on my face.

Baby Girl is reenacting the moments leading up to the fire: she cradles her sketchpad against her chest with one hand, she flicks her other hand against her brown thighs like flames.

Nobody asks how it started. Not the cop that gets on the radio trying to find us a place to sleep, not the firefighters that come two engines strong and exhaust both water reservoirs on the slow, endless trickle of gas feeding what eventually is just a glowing-red frame of a car we don't recognize. As far as we know the car could burn forever, because when we pull off with the cop in search of a hotel, Baby Girl sitting shotgun, me stuck in back behind the partition, the firefighters are still wiping their brows from the unrelenting heat.

The cop and Baby Girl discuss what to do next, where we should go, but I can't hear much because of the partition, so I cringe and put my face as close as I can without kissing the grease, spit, and drunk blood dried to the bullet-proof glass. "Holiday Inn," I yell.

The cop turns, yells back, "The rooms are all filled with evacuees still. But don't worry. We'll find something. It may take awhile. But we'll find something."

Baby Girl reaches in her back pocket and pulls out the photo of her and the trumpet blower. She puts it at the top of the drawing, pushing it in between the bound papers. She sharpens her charcoal with her dad's old Buck knife and then goes to work, shading in the base of her nose.

I think the cop says, Nice knife.

Baby Girl turns around and knocks on the partition. "Stop pouting. Get your head off the window!"

"Being back here, I've been thinking. With all this talk, you know, starting anew, I think tomorrow, when the hangover wears off, I should take the first steps to get my record expunged."

The cop turns to Baby Girl. "Record?" he says.

Baby Girl puts her hand on the cop's shoulder, smearing her charcoal all over his stripes. "Minor charges, sir. Drunk and disorderly."

Baby Girl is a good liar, not that she is good at lying, but when she does lie it's for a good cause. I do have an assault charge and that isn't fair. I had skipped my court date. Baby Girl told me she agrees with me that it's not fair, but she probably just says that because she doesn't want to hurt my feelings. Lately, she says less and less of the kinds of things I'd wish she'd say to me, but she doesn't have to because we both know it doesn't matter at this point.

"All that aside, sir, money isn't an issue right now. If we could just get a room," I say.

"Or a rental car. That would be cheaper and we could still get home tonight. Is there a rental place open now?" Baby Girl says.

"It's too late," the cop says.

"You sure? Not a Hertz or anything around?" she says.

The cop says nothing. I can tell Baby Girl doesn't want to drag out the trip any longer. I start to wonder if she even plans on spending that first night with me back home.

We slow and pull up to a motel with a walk-up window. There's a locked, rusted gate in front of the office door. The glow of a Coke machine casts a light on a condom dispenser that accepts quarters only. I notice the picture of Baby Girl and the trumpet blower taped to the top of the sketchpad. It's starting to curl at the edges as if protesting.

"You know it's only ten. I'd think we could get a rental now." Baby Girl flips the cover of her sketchpad closed. "We can still get home tonight."

"This Hattiesburg, lady. The only twenty-four hours we got here are the truck stops. And all the hotels are booked with FEMA. Now I got the dispatcher trying to find y'all a spot to sleep. When was that D and D charge, young man?" The cop starts typing on his dash computer.

"Either 2004 or 5," I say. I'm honest with him. At this point, who cares? It might be better off if he just takes me in and Baby Girl can just go on without me. A clean break.

"Don't mean to be a bad host during your unplanned stop in my town, but I'm not in the business of helping criminals," the cop says.

I see an unlit reader board announcing "Hourly Rates." Baby Girl, in a manner that stops me from losing my temper, keeps shading the bridge of her nose in the drawing. Her light brown hair, glowing more than usual because of the parking lot lights shining in from overhead, hangs down over her face so neither I nor the cop can see her face.

The cop keeps punching keys on his computer.

"Well, while you're doing that I'm going to see about rooms," she says to the cop. She flips her sketchpad closed and gets out of the cruiser.

I try to follow her but my door's locked. I slide over and try the other door. "Sir, can you let me out?"

"Sit tight, bud. The lady can check on the room," the cop says, still punching keys on his computer.

His screen flashes a red "Error" message. He gets on his radio. "Dispatch, can you run a warrant check in the Orleans Parish database?"

"Negative, system is down," a voice mutters back.

"They got rooms!" Baby Girl yells.

"You lucked out for now, bud." The cop gets out of his cruiser and opens my door for me. "Welcome to Hattiesburg. I'll see y'all around."

I know cop bullshit when I hear it so I just ignore him. I get our bags and struggle up to Baby Girl and the clerk's window.

"I told him we wanted to stay till six. I want to get out of here as soon as the sun rises," Baby Girl says.

Shaved shag nylon carpeting, yellow but browned with footprints, fills the air in the motel room with the smell of dust and bad sex. I put our bags on top of the dresser, afraid that the odor will seep into our only possessions if they touch the floor.

"I don't think we should take our socks off," I say.

"No. And I'm sleeping in my clothes," Baby Girl says.

She smiles at me as she searches through her bag. She pulls out her toothbrush and walks over to the sink.

"Sorry, hun. But I think we're going to be the first couple ever to make an honest establishment out of this dump," she says.

"Unfortunately, I agree."

She turns, scrubbing, drooling a little bit of foamy Colgate onto the counter. "Open the curtains and crack the window. I want the sunrise to wake us up."

My cell rings. Thibodeaux asks me where we are. "What?" he yells over the music. It's even louder than the last time I talked to him.

I'm so tired I just tell him that the car broke down, that we're coming in tomorrow. "Happy birthday," he says. "I'd come get you, but I started celebrating hours ago."

We start for Waffle House at dawn, lumbering with decaffeinated steps as our ill-fitting backpacks bounce against the tops of our asses. Baby Girl struggles to keep her sketchpad up under her right arm, her fingertips just barely able to reach and support its other end. We had seen the Waffle House back near I-59, about four miles down the road. After eating breakfast, we would search for a rental car.

"You want me to carry that?" I ask her.

"No. Just walk faster," she says.

As the sun warms the grass, the humidity surges and I feel my back get wet with sweat. Baby Girl stops and puts her sketchpad down so she can tie up her hair with a yellow rubber band. She sees me watching her.

"What?" she says.

"Why isn't it us?" I say, pointing at the drawing.

She wipes her forehead with her arm. "You mean, why isn't it you, right?"

That shuts me up. Real quick. Like now I feel like an ass for asking, real quick.

"Come on," she says. "You're just slowing us down with that

nonsense."

"Nonsense?" I say. But she just keeps walking.

The hotel parking lots all around us stay full with cars. The guests have nowhere to go. Maybe some will find the optimism to get up and drive home to start gutting their houses. They could give us a ride. We could pay for the gas.

"We could hitchhike?" I say.

"But then we'd be stuck there without a car. It's going to be harder to get a rental car back home," Baby Girl says.

I guess I had figured things would just be better when we got there. It's got to be better than this.

Just then an old burgundy LeBaron with some of that fake wood side paneling creeps up next to us, the driver's side of the car slumping dangerously close to the road. Bass rattling the rusted trunk, the car squeaks to a slow stop ahead of us. I see a huge man sitting in the front seat.

"I'm going to tell him we'd like a ride to Waffle House." Baby Girl walks up to the passenger side window.

As the LeBaron window rolls down the treble explodes David Banner lyrics and duets with the bass-rattling trunk, so that I can't hear what Baby Girl is saying to what looks like a giant sitting in the front seat. She's smiling, leaning against the door. Then laughing, Baby Girl stands up straight and waves for me to hurry up.

"I can take you to Waffle House!" this fat black dude hollers out at me. He's big, like unhealthy big. He's busting at the seams all over the place, all over the emergency brake in the middle of the front seats, up against the steering wheel, his belly and tits can't be held back by the seatbelt. A green oxygen tank sits on the passenger side floor, the tube running from it feeds into the fat guy's nostrils. A collection of prescription medication is scattered across the dashboard.

Baby Girl is grinning, showing all her straight little teeth. "Great, right!"

After a bit of a struggle to reach the lever down by his knees, the big dude pops the trunk. I cram the bags in against the shivering subwoofers. Baby Girl, getting in the front seat, lifts her leg up to avoid the oxygen tank and eases herself down onto the cracked brown leather interior.

"It ain't a thing. Just right down the road…" I think the big dude says.

We start creeping down the highway at about thirty per hour. The bass, so early in the morning, puts me on edge and then I see that cop drive right by us going in the opposite direction. Baby Girl slowly turns and watches the cop.

"Yeah, we need to get out of here. No offense, but this town gives me the creeps," Baby Girl yells over the music.

The fat guy pushes the mute button on his in-dash and the treble fades away and the bass bubbles down from a hard buzz to a calm rumble, like we just left a thunderstorm somewhere behind us.

"Where y'all going?"

"We were on our way back but had some car trouble and got stranded here," Baby Girl says.

"Stranded? Yep, things sure been a fuck-storm pretty much everywhere down here. My name is Antoine DuMonde."

"DuMonde?" I say.

"Yeah, sort of a nickname. Just call me Antoine."

We don't go above thirty per hour. Antoine takes the music off mute and allows it to bang and massage my back while the letters of the Waffle House sign ahead of us slowly grow bigger and bigger like batter blowing up out of an iron.

Baby Girl slaps the photo down on Antoine's dash as if calling her seat for good. She goes to work on her chin.

Antoine nods down against his bloated neck. "Pretty

picture," he yells over the music.

"Thanks. Almost there."

He rolls down the window. "Hey girl, you mind turning that thing up a little more for me?"

Baby Girl lifts her sketchpad off the tank and turns the oxygen up. Antoine takes a few deep breaths.

"Thanks, girl."

"You alright, Antoine?" I ask.

"Naw, not really. I mean do I look alright to you?"

"Not at all," I mumble.

"I just got out of the hospital, man. Motherfuckers shoved me back in my car after I stabilized. I don't feel stabilized. But they say they're too crowded with all these people running inland to deal with a lost cause like me."

"Jesus, Antoine. They really said that?" I say.

"Yeah, some young white boy look like you. All upset and yelling about how it all unfair. I thought to myself, I didn't need to come to a hospital for some white boy to tell me I'm fucked because I'm poor and black."

Baby Girl lifts up her pad to Antoine. "Does that look like my chin?"

"Hell yeah, it does," he says.

"What about the guy's chin?" she says.

"It doesn't look sweaty enough."

Baby Girl hangs back over the drawing.

"I mean they didn't say it like that but it was clear. Boy, what planet are you from?" He's smiling at me through his rearview mirror. "Shit's fucked up around here. Some sick nigga isn't a thing!"

The car bottoms out with our weight, wheels moaning against the wells, as Antoine eases us into the Waffle House parking lot. An eerie quiet wakes me from my daze when Antoine turns the car off and the music stops suddenly. I can hear the rush of cars on the overpass above us. Baby Girl and I get out, shut our doors. Antoine opens his door, but he doesn't budge.

"I need to catch my breath. I'll chill here," he says.

I walk around and see his swollen legs. They're wrapped with bandages browned with dried blood. He catches me staring.

"Bedsores," he says.

Baby Girl orders two grilled cheeses, three coffees, one waffle and three servings of scrambled eggs to go. When they bring our food to us in Styrofoam, Baby Girl takes the coffee mug out the door with her too.

The waitress waves at us as we walk outside. "Ah, screw it," I hear her say.

We sit down on the pavement by Antoine's open car door. "Y'all didn't have to do that," he says.

"It stinks like burnt bacon in there," I say.

Antoine and I tear into our grilled cheeses. Baby Girl picks up her waffle with her right hand, the one that doesn't have charcoal all over it, and eats the waffle plain. I try not to look at Antoine's legs as I eat. I feel the gravel on the pavement plant itself in my legs so that when I change my position little rocks and grit stick in my skin.

"What's next?" Antoine asks.

"Rent a car, I guess," I say.

"We're getting home today," Baby Girl says.

"You're going to have a hard time finding a car to rent. I bet you they're all taken, or gone."

"I mean, we can try," Baby Girl says.

"I'll drive you to some places, but I'm telling you, they're all gone," Antoine says.

Baby Girl takes our Styrofoam containers and dumps them in the trashcan. Antoine reaches for some medication from his dashboard and then lets out a bit of a moan with his effort. He looks at the pill and then he throws it on the floor of his car. He explains how it makes his stomach hurt, and how the blood thinners make him get light-headed all the time, so he barely ever takes the stuff, which is another reason why the doctors are tired of him clogging up their schedules.

We get back on the highway and head down to a Hertz. The sun, now high and strong, is making Antoine drip with sweat. He wipes his face with a white hand towel. My ass is sticking to the leather seat and Baby Girl is leaning at an angle towards the window so the wind catches her hair. She uses the oxygen tank as a sort of easel for her sketchpad.

We pull into Hertz. Baby Girl says she wants to keep working on her drawing. The parking lot is empty except for one car so I walk in expecting to just walk right back out. "No. We haven't had anything for some time now," the woman behind the desk tells me without turning from her show. "We're under contract with insurance adjusters. It's like that everywhere." She turns to me and adds, "I'd be real surprised if you found anything."

So I walk right back out.

Antoine is taking loud deep breaths through his nose, pointing at Baby Girl's drawing. "I like that there. But make your cheeks a bit rounder, like how you're smiling in the photo."

"Nothing?" Baby Girl asks, using her charcoal-covered hand to shield the sun from her eyes.

"Lady said there isn't anything anywhere," I say.

"I believe her." Antoine gasps. "Turn that up again, would ya?"

"Well, we should try another place," Baby Girl says as she turns up the oxygen.

"I don't know if it's worth it. What about a bus station?"

"Listen y'all. I need to get back home. I'm going to die right here if I don't get home and sit in my A/C. I've driven you around. Now let me go home. If you help me get back in my house I'll get somebody to take you to the bus station."

"Can you just drop us off at the bus station?" I ask.

"I wish. But it isn't that easy. Like I said, I think I need help getting out of this car and back in my house."

Antoine talks about how bad the bedsores got in the hospital. He sat neglected while trying to recover from a heart attack. His sister in Pensecola had her own problems to deal with. She wouldn't come up and help. When he was discharged, the nurses had helped him into his car and never looked back. They threw an oxygen tank in the front seat and said good luck. And then they lied, You'll be fine, Antoine. And he lied, Of course I will. It surely wasn't legal, but I guess it was the way to do things after so many other people had already been left to die.

The bass is back. Still thumping with a kind of power that seems impossible for this old LeBaron. Boom-boom. Thirty per hour, we drive into some abandoned farmlands with gnarly rusted barb and termite-eaten posts. Boom-boom. We pull into the dirt driveway of a house that has an unfinished wooden door and a porch with all the screens busted and hanging into the azaleas. Boom-boom. Antoine slowly pulls the car onto the lawn so his driver's side is at the foot of the steps. Boom. He shuts the car off.

He tells us that we have to move the oxygen tank into the house first. "By the time y'all get me to the couch, I'm going to be huffing and puffing."

The tank, which is three feet tall, probably weighs about sixty pounds. The humidity and our lack of good sleep make it heavier. We set the tank down by the couch. I notice an old and faded blue eviction notice stuck to the front door of the house.

Antoine waits in the LeBaron. We try three times before Baby Girl and I finally get him on his feet and leaning against his walker. My head is lost in his left armpit and Baby Girl is grunting from his right armpit. Our legs, quivering and wobbling at the knees, get him up one step at a time. We kick magazines and clothes out of the way as we go through his living room. When he falls back onto the couch we hear a support crack somewhere, maybe in the couch, maybe in the floor.

Baby Girl places the tubes up to his nose and I crank the oxygen. We wait in silence, other than our heavy breathing, for Antoine to catch his breath and speak. "Go to the-" he pauses, swallows. "Go into my bedroom. In the top right drawer there's a folder. Get it."

Antoine reaches behind himself and flips the A/C unit on. Baby Girl is filling up a glass of water as I walk back to the bedroom.

His bed doesn't look like it's been slept in for a long time. The sheets, despite their brown and dusty appearance, are folded up neatly on top of the bare mattress. I find the folder.

Antoine grabs the folder from me and flips through a collection of papers. He hands Baby Girl the registration and title to the LeBaron. "Go home."

Baby Girl smiles. "You serious?"

"Wait, Antoine. We can't just take your car, man," I say.

"All I want is the drawing. It's a fair trade. Shit, that car isn't worth more than three hundred. You'll be lucky if you even make it."

"Let me give you some cash at least for it."

Baby Girl walks out the door and I hear her go down the front steps. I follow her.

"I got so many hospital bills a little cash isn't going to do a damn thing for me. If the girl gives me the drawing, I'm giving her the car," Antoine yells after me.

"This doesn't seem right," I say, chasing after Baby Girl.

She's slowly tearing the drawing from the sketchpad.

"This is a bum deal," I say. "Are you going to let him do this?"

"Are you *not* going to let him do this?" Baby Girl tears out the drawing. "Listen, I want to get home. Do you?"

"Yeah, of course."

"Well, then act like it." She hands me the drawing. "We need to do something. You need to do something."

We both know Antoine's lying when he says that he'll be okay. And we know he's lying when he says we'll be okay. "Shit will be ugly down there, but you'll be just fine. Don't drive faster than forty-five. The front wheels are way out of alignment. Now shut the door and get out of here, you're wasting my A/C."

We leave him sitting on his couch, the drawing of Baby Girl and the trumpet blower next to him. The bass line beats Boom-Boom again as we find our way back to I-59.

Forty-five per hour south. The sun starts to set. Then we see the Bienvenue sign. Then we cross the lake. The smell of decay cuts through the humid wind. Baby Girl looks out over the water and then at the city skyline. "Jesus Christ, I feel so lonely," she says out the window. But I don't say a word. We don't say a word to each other.

DISASTER RELIEF

Thibodeaux stands by a mini charcoal grill flipping some preformed burger patties in the courtyard of our favorite bar. The flames against his hunched frame create a shadow on the water-stained wall behind him, and the shadow dances with Patsy Cline's *Back in Baby's Arms* as the song plays through the one speaker still working in the bar. A couple months ago Thibodeaux was working sous-chef at a damn fine restaurant and making some of the best redfish almondene in the city.

Baby Girl is stuck eating one of the burger patties, but she still does it pretty and clean, manicured pinkies up in casual dainty and a paper towel resting on her brown thighs and the frays of her cut-off jean shorts.

"You could make a turd taste good, Thibodeaux!" she yells. Then she sees me staring at her thighs, and lets me for a moment. When we'd lived at her mom's house, I'd been nervous about looking at her and touching her. Now I look at her every chance I get. She lifts up my chin and stuffs a piece of burger in my mouth, the kind of intimate gesture I'd missed for a while now.

Our first day back and the tap water's too infested to wash your hands before you eat. We'd been warned that the Sewerage Board was shocking the water supply with high amounts of chlorine to kill bacteria, been warned not to take showers, not to brush teeth, but sometimes you'd forget and out of habit you'd stick your hands under a faucet and then your cuticles would burn and you'd remember. It's a hard thing to get used to, not washing your hands with tap water, which is why Thibodeaux is constantly putting lotion on his ashy hands to soothe the burning. Sanitizer gives some reassurance. It's no good for cleaning actual dirt off your hands, but with all the garbage and stinking refrigerators sitting on the curbs, it's nice to know that there's a giant, pump-dispensing bottle of Purell sitting on the bar next to two pump-dispensing bottles of catsup and mustard. The mayonnaise is in the trashcan.

If things were anything like normal, the courtyard would be full of people, maybe Andrei would ask me to feel the nylon-clad thigh of the young woman next to him. I'd politely decline, but then he'd keep prodding me to do it until I'd submit and touch the girl's thigh. The nylon would feel smooth enough that I'd almost put my head in her lap right then and there, and the girl would smile, or not.

"I didn't know they made 'em this big," I say, pumping some of the Purell on my palm.

"Yeah. Got a bunch of 'em for free from volunteers," Thibodeaux yells from the courtyard.

Last time I'd seen Thibodeaux I was picking him up at a gas station in BR after his car broke down. He had called his girlfriend from the payphone, but she'd refused to accept the collect-call charges and hung up. On the ride back, stuck in traffic, I'd tried convincing him that she'd come around. I'd said something cheesy and useless like, "That's what sucks about love, you become a victim of her stupidity and, worse usually, she becomes a victim of your stupidity."

There was a time—it's hard to imagine it now—when Baby Girl and I had conversations with friends we honestly loved, really loved. Some of these friends we loved were people we never met, or don't remember, but if you were there anytime before, you might understand that foolish sentiment.

When Baby Girl and I came back we drove across the connection and a pungent aroma intensified as we neared the city and exited the interstate under the shadow of what was a coliseum. The warped doors tried to keep us from entering the cottage we rented and seeing the fallen insulation, the black mold seemed to heave and wheeze as it spread over our artwork, our couch, and the clothes that we had worn just a couple months ago when we would have danced to anything.

While at Baby Girl's mom's house we didn't have sex because we didn't want to disrespect her mom, or maybe we were just too disoriented to lie still enough together, but even after coming back home we couldn't. "Maybe we should just ignore the fallen ceiling and shingles on our bed," Baby Girl said.

Our clothes, still stuck on the floor and covered in the mold that continues to spread through our home, got drenched in our sweat the week before we had to evacuate. Some trumpeter was busting out some crazy shit, and in between sets he played some local rap off his iPod and kept us all jumping during trips to the bar and back to the dance floor. Baby Girl and I danced; I held her belly as it grew with beans and cake and booze right up until the last song. I'd used so much Tabasco that I couldn't feel her lips when she would kiss me. Those were nights when home was a slow bike ride to a place where my head rested on her bicep and my nose on the top of her breast, where I could smell the sweaty fun she'd had that night. That was it: just fun and sleep.

Whenever she would leave me alone in the city for a while, and I never bothered to ask where she went, I'd find myself comparing things in the city to her: her legs and the long limbs of the live oaks and how their roots upend the sidewalks, the smell of the streetcar braking and the smell of her hair after biking home from work. Eventually, the city and Baby Girl became the same affair.

Now, we're riding a big, dirty wave of great loss and pending opportunity into what seems like a rebirth conceived with no expectations. We *are* sure that our fridge is dead, the chicken, pork and catfish inside it long rotten; maggots dine on what remains and frame the inside of the fridge like cake icing. Tomorrow, we'll have to move the fridge to the curb. Our old Japanese cars, humble transportation to the jobs we took for granted, are encrusted with the stank that regurgitated from the sewers and into the streets. A blue tarp lies on the roof of our house, stretched tight and weighed down with bricks in a pathetic attempt to keep out any future rain.

Thibodeaux comes into the bar from the courtyard and grabs a beer from the ice chest. "Yours will be done in a bit," he says to me. The scars on Thibodeaux's arms and wrists always give me a bit of a chill, but he once got laid by a chick that was into his cooking scars. She was actually turned on by them; she made a point to say that New Orleans cooking scars made her wet. The day after she had bathed Thibodeaux's scars in kisses and bodily fluids, he met me on top of the levee so we could take in the sun and watch the tankers come and go from the refineries.

"Is it the scars she likes, or just the fact that you're a cook?" I asked.

"She said she likes scars from cooking here, this city only. Scars from cooking in other cities don't do a damn thing for her. See that one right there?" Thibodeaux pointed at a welt of skin rising off his wrist like an albino leech. "I got that one from some dumbass fry cook on a cruise ship a couple years ago, he threw some oysters in a fryer all sloppy right as I was walking by and I got hit by some oil. That was a shit job. And that scar did nothing for her. And here's the thing, I never told her it wasn't a New Orleans-cooking scar, but she sensed it somehow. Skipped right over the damn thing when she was kissing my hands and wrists. I even tried to convince her that I got it working at Commander's. She just squinted at it and said 'No,' that it made her 'dry as a desert.' But when she found this one from Delmonico's—I'd gotten a little sloppy when I had to help a line cook rush some prep." He pointed at a large scar on his other wrist. "This one. When she got her lips on it, it was as if all the levees failed at the same time! A great summertime flood, bra!"

If there's an acronym for a fetish in New Orleans-cooking scars, Thibodeaux's *T* would be the first letter. Despite that, he's not much of a romantic, but more of a caretaker, which is why he keeps post back in the courtyard by his shitty little grill, cooking that shitty little burger for me. Baby Girl and I could always get an excellent meal from Thibodeaux. Even during times when you're lucky to get an MRE—constipation—from the Red Cross, I bet Thibodeaux could keep us eating something that still makes food feel like a lifestyle.

"He looks lonely out there by himself," Baby Girl says.

"I think he looks content."

Thibodeaux stares at the flames with a frown, poking that cheap patty.

A dull crunching sound comes over the music, and as we dwell on Thibodeaux's decline from sous-chef at one of the best restaurants in the city to grill cook at a shuttered French Quarter bar, that water-stained wall behind our lonely cook comes spilling down, flooding the courtyard with rotted wood and knocking over the grill. My burger patty, caked in dust and lead paint chips, sits in the rubble.

"Really?" Thibodeaux yells. "Really! It's okay, it's okay. I'll get you fed, bra!" He points at me, wading through the rubble as he charges back into the bar. He lifts up an ice chest and walks back to the courtyard where he dumps the melting ice all over the coals.

He stands, surrounded by the smoke and the bubbling ash at his feet, and he investigates the fallen wall. "This was bound to happen eventually!" he yells. "But the framing looks fine."

I hear him, but I don't really think about it. Baby Girl squeezes my thigh. And I know she wants me to get Thibodeaux to stop and just sit with us.

"Thibodeaux, it's okay, man. I'm not that hungry anyway," I say.

"No, bra. You gotta eat."

"I got some peanut butter and bread back in my suitcase. He'll be fine," Baby Girl says. She walks behind the bar and grabs a broom and a dustpan.

Thibodeaux rushes back behind the bar and looks through another ice chest. He picks up a greasy freezer bag filled with brown ground beef and sniffs at it. "Shit stinks." He slams the lid down on the ice chest and moves down, opening another. "Yesterday's meat's no good." He shakes the oily water off his hand.

Baby Girl hands me the dustpan. "Get off your butt," she says.

"Thibodeaux, don't worry about it, man," I say. I get up and follow Baby Girl to the courtyard, dragging a trashcan behind me.

A big change is coming, that's what Baby Girl and I tell each other, and that's what makes us bike home from Molly's to sleep for the first time since coming back home, like if we sleep, maybe it will all change overnight.

The Quarter is quiet, so quiet we hear the hum of our tires on the asphalt. There are no horse-drawn carriages clopping down the street or drunken tourists yelling with temporary might from shitty mixed drinks. We pedal down Governor

Nichols swerving down the street to St. Claude Ave. As we slow our approach to Rampart we see two green Humvees crawling towards us. We continue to cross until spotlights on top of the military trucks blind us. I shade my eyes.

"They're stopping," Baby Girl says and starts coasting her bike.

I think to myself that I don't understand martial law. I don't know what it allows these people to do to us. Seems to me it just gives them more room to fuck up and then not be held accountable, that we can be made to look as if we asked for whatever bad shit happens to us, because we like to dance until the early morning, or because we spend too much time on food, or because we look forward to Lent as long as we can.

We slow our bikes and rest our feet on the pavement, watching as the Humvees cut us off with a half-circle formation. Two soldiers climb out of one of the Humvees and point their guns at our feet. We hold our handlebars.

A voice barks through a loudspeaker, demanding IDs and telling us we're violating curfew. The soldiers don't say a word but continue pointing their guns at our feet. I decide they're National Guard. It's obvious from their double chins and the awkward grasps on their weapons that their monthly training requirements haven't prepared them for what's happening here.

"We're just on our way home," I yell at the tinted windows. "We were hungry and can't cook in our kitchen."

"You need to eat at midnight?" one of the soldiers says.

"It's none of your damned business when I want to eat," I say. I'm pissed and I've had some usual beers, but I never expected that everything would go perfect. But when did time start mattering so much?

"Hun, take it easy," Baby Girl says, shaking her head.

Another soldier, sitting shotgun in the leading Humvee, gets out, unarmed, and walks towards us. "We're here for your protection. There're a lot of stolen guns floating around here. You understand? Lots of people with guns." He says it slowly, with a Midwest accent, as if I don't speak the same language.

"Like you guys?" I say.

"Put a bracelet on him," he says.

One of the soldiers swings his weapon around to his back and grabs my arm. He throws me to the ground with my bike still in between my legs; he pulls my arms behind me and I feel the gravel and dirt grind against my lips, and it all tastes metallic like blood. I scream. I hear Baby Girl beg them to stop. I hear a zip and feel plastic cut tightly into my wrists.

"Up!" the soldier says and pulls at my arms. He throws me into the back of a Humvee and slams the door shut. I yell, ask why I'm under arrest. The eyes of the soldier sitting behind the wheel keep a steady, unblinking gaze on me. "Nobody ever said you were under arrest," he says and laughs.

I see Baby Girl looking at me and I press my forehead against the window, I feel helpless, trying to hear what they're saying to her. The superior walks to the passenger side and gets in. The soldiers outside tighten their circle around Baby Girl; she just keeps staring at me, not saying anything. By the look on her face I can't tell if she's scared or just pissed at me. I don't think she's scared. I can't hear what they're saying to her. And if Baby Girl said something, I wouldn't be able to hear her. I want her to tell me something, and thinking about what she might tell me calms me down. "Hey, son!" the superior says, turning to look at me. "If she was to go back to that wrecked-to-all-hell home by herself tonight, and you couldn't do anything about it, how would that make you feel?" He takes off his cap and rubs his crew cut.

"She'd be okay," I say immediately.

He starts running my name and I know I'm fucked at that point.

"You sure you feel that way? Because with the crazies running around this city and with all that filth festering in your home I'd bet you'd worry about that pretty girl. Imagine the things that would want her," he says.

When the warrant for my arrest comes up he puts in a call for somebody to come escort Baby Girl home. I yell as they drive me away.

I sit in an encampment for two weeks before being taken to BR. It's a month or so before Thibodeaux gets me out. On the ride back down I-10, he says he saw Baby Girl in the Bywater.

"She was drinking some wine on the stoop of some gutjob. Taking a break from working on it. Still had her gloves on." He stops for second and turns his attention from the road to look at me. "We talked a bit," he says. "I think she went in on it with a friend or something."

"Where's the house?" I said.

"Fat chance, bra. No way in hell."

"Yeah, asshole? Why tell me anything then?"

"Cause that's where K— is and you should know there's nothing you can do about it."

For a while, I have a hard time wrapping my head around her leaving without a word; I refuse to admit there wasn't something left to say. But at night, when the power cuts in and out and I'm sitting on my porch drinking, waiting for Thibodeaux to get off work and staring at that broken down LeBaron and my snot-covered Camry, the stuckness of it all, I think I know why she said she was lonely, and I drift in and out of sleep, tired from cleaning all day, and I think I see her in a brief moment of blurry consciousness. When Thibodeaux stops by for a nightcap after work and gives me a kick to wake me up, the LeBaron is gone.

And this is the thing I try to stop myself from doing: Sometimes I think about what it would have been like if I had gone home with her that night. I don't like to think that everything would have been okay. But I do like to think that I could have had just one more night, or one more week, if I was really lucky.

Under the vigil of St. Augustine's rusted iron and concrete steeple outside our window, I had watched Baby Girl, wearing shorts only, stand at the window and do a charcoal sketch of the steeple. The rust on the cast iron had ran with warm rain down the sides of the steeple, staining the old, painted concrete like eyeliner running down the cheeks of a widow. Baby Girl lightly brushed the charcoal down the drawing with her index finger to show the tears.

If I had gone home with her that night, we would have walked our bikes through the gate in front of our house and rested them on top of each other. I'd climb our stoop and open the front door; she'd lock the bikes together to the small crepe myrtle tree in the yard. Inside our house, the air would be thick with the smell of mold. I'd open the front windows and walk back outside, complaining about the smell.

I'd walk around to the side of the house and reach for the aluminum ladder underneath. I'd try to pull it out but it would get stuck on something so I'd start jerking at it until I'd lose my grip.

I would stand up and for the first time, I'd cry. She'd wrap her arms around me and laugh at me a little bit. And it would feel good to hear her laugh at me and I'd forget that I'm crying.

She'd let go of me and squat down with her hands on her knees, looking at the ladder with no haste. I'd help her pull the ladder out, and I'd stand it against the side of our house.

I'd have a feeling we're Louis Prima and Keely Smith reincarnated. I'd climb up the ladder and grab a corner of the big blue tarp on our roof. Baby Girl would holler as I pull with what strength I have and send the tarp cascading into the front yard.

On the air mattress, we'd agree to make love one last time because why not. The stars and the steeple would watch us through the holes in our roof, and we'd hear the banana trees in the backyard applaud our performance, and maybe we would.

"Do you want me to tell you it gets better?" Baby Girl would ask.

I'd tell her, No, but she would do it anyway. I'd breathe in the humidity and I swear I'd smell the scent of the jasmine vines blooming instead of mold.

TWO

NAUMAN'S INSTALLATION

I'm standing on the veranda overlooking the Chicago Art Institute's contemporary wing. The ledge induces vertigo, which I welcome as temporary relief from my work-study assignment. Then three construction workers push a wall on a dolly out of the freight elevator, through the lobby, and into what was a William Eggleston exhibit. More workers follow behind them with more walls on dollies. My radio crackles to life, interrupting my reverie in this dizziness, and the head of security summons me to the curator's office to receive the details of my new assignment. The stairwell acoustics amplify my labored climb up the stone, six flights.

("Does it bother you that I don't ask how work is going?"

"No. You know what happens. The best parts are after I leave and before I go back.")

The curator and the head of security stand in front of a laptop, its screen reflects off their glasses. They both look up and then back down at the screen, and the head of security waves me over. I walk behind the two and peer over their shoulders at the computer screen.

Bruce Nauman, in a bed, with the tubes for oxygen cluttering his image through Skype video, instructs the curator not to place warning signs around the installation that he had titled *Second Poem Piece*. "Please, I don't want any sort of unintended distraction around this piece. Please." He hacks and then wipes phlegm from his lips. A nurse enters the picture and says that

Mr. Nauman cannot speak any longer, at the moment. "He needs rest." The nurse ends the video feed.

The curator turns to me. "There will be no signs warning guests about Mr. Nauman's art in the floor. You alone will watch over the installation," he says.

"And do not let anybody step on it," says the head of security.

"Do not let anybody step on the installation," says the curator. "That's settled. Now, I must reorganize the south wing. Go to the Nauman piece."

"Is Nauman dying?" I ask. As if I know the guy.

"You know him? I mean, his work?" the curator asks.

"No," I say.

There are corridors and wings of the museum that confuse me and then change and confuse me for the first time. I get lost frequently, if not because of the maze of walls then because the curator is constantly changing the order of the walls and the art that they exhibit. Pollock was once where I got my cue to turn right for Nauman, but now there is a giant painting of an open mouth, by whom I'm not intrigued, and I can't turn right; now there is a wall with a giant painting of an eye. There was a bathroom down the hall where I used to take a right and I wonder if the bathroom is still there. The curator couldn't reroute plumbing that quickly, I decide. There must be a new entryway leading to the bathroom, to the right.

I run into another security guard, a pudgy little white man named Sam, and ask him for directions. "This is the new map," Sam says, pulling out a rough copy of the contemporary art wing's latest layout. "Go through the Penskat exhibit, then the Reynolds exhibit and then the Walker exhibit and you'll get to Nauman."

"None of that sounds familiar," I say.

"Here then. Take my map. I'll be fine." Sam walks off then stops and walks behind a movie screen, which is showing projection video of a car garage that opens slowly, a man exits pushing a lawnmower toward a yard overwhelmed by tall dandelions. I can see Sam's feet below the movie screen as he stands behind it.

"Sam?" I say.

"I like seeing dandelions sway backwards in the wind," he says.

("I don't have a lot of luck with plants. I just don't have an angel watching over me."

"I blame this weather. But either way, having an angel watch over you might not be as nice as you'd think.")

Nauman ordered the sixty-by-sixty-inch steel plaque to be placed in the museum's hardwood floor, leveled with the floor's surface. He had stamped the words YOU, MAY, NOT, WANT, TO, SCREW, HERE (or HEAR) in vertical columns, creating different combinations of the words in horizontal rows.

"Ma'am, don't step on the artwork," I say, and shift my weight from my left foot to my right foot. I want to lean back against the wall and relax but I don't because I worry that people won't take me seriously.

"How is anybody supposed to know this is artwork?" the lady whispers, but real audibly, to the old man next to her. The old man is holding what I assume is the lady's purse. I've done that before. There have been times when I appreciated holding a purse. I want people to take me seriously.

("When is Muses this year?"
    "Same as every year.")

There's a constant knocking sound too, like from a pendulum: the exhibit in the next room shows black and white footage of a tall skinny white guy, Nauman in his youth, tapping, barefoot, the corners of a white box marked on a concrete floor, and he's tapping in time with the knocking. The video loops, but you'd never know from here because all you hear is a seamless knocking sound. It doesn't pause, not even when the video loops back to the beginning. But I assume it has a beginning, that Nauman started somewhere.

These are times I feel like I got the dumbest job in the world. Everybody thinks this stuff is ridiculous. Everybody wonders why they don't just have a sign warning people, why this plaque's not on the wall like most artwork, or why this stupid guy is standing here waiting to warn people right when they're about to step on the thing.

"Sir, please don't step on the artwork."

Most of the time, I can tell if someone is the type of person that would step on the artwork if I didn't interrupt. They usually enter, their eyes searching the walls, and walk toward the installation wondering where that knocking sound is coming from. If I take immediate action and tell people to not step on the artwork as soon as they enter the exhibit, I look like an asshole and some other asshole will say that he would have seen the installation and would have never been dumb enough to step on it. So, to avoid insulting anybody, I wait until the person is taking the one last stride that makes their stepping on Nauman's Installation inevitable unless I say something. Then I say something. And when I do say something the person usually backpedals, laughs with some sort of embarrassment, and looks at me like I'm the one that put Nauman there in the floor.

Nauman's Installation is right around the corner of a wall separating it from the next exhibit, so that when someone comes around the wall they're right on top of the installation. The curator's layout forces them to walk right on it like a welcome mat.

"Sir, don't step on the artwork."

It's discouraging to know that art invokes such a repetitious reaction from its audience. I would never argue that puzzlement is weak inspiration because it doesn't lead to any instant gratification. Never.

"I don't get the point of this. It's pointless. There's no point. Let's go see the fucking Seurat exhibit," a man weighed down by an oversized Red Sox sweatshirt says to an elderly woman in a wheelchair.

I love instant gratification. I just realized that.

("What do you do when you can't sleep?"
"I say, "Give up on the day!"")

There are eighteen different combinations of Nauman's words, including the possibilities that involve the removal of words. But after standing here, guarding it from the crud people track in on their shoes, I've gotten comfortable enough to convince myself that there have to be more combinations than that.

"Sir, don't step on the artwork."

"Why'd you put it in the floor?"

"I didn't put it in the floor. I'm just paying for my tuition."

"You know what I meant. Do you hear that knocking noise? What is that?"

"I haven't heard anything for a while."

I have a surprisingly easy time believing this, even when I swear that knocking noise from the video exhibit next door gets louder.

"You don't hear that?" he says, throwing a hand in the direction of the next exhibit.

"No. Ladies, excuse me. Ladies, please don't step on the art."

The man is not convinced that I don't hear the noise, I guess, because he just keeps staring at me.

"Ladies and gentlemen," I say, waving my arms slowly to get their attention. "Please exit the exhibit so that the museum can perform maintenance. It will reopen momentarily. This is all routine."

I pull a velvet rope across the entrance and wait for the last person to leave the exhibit. "It'll be just a minute," I say.

On my way back to the lobby I get turned around. The map is no longer current. I stop to admire a large black and white photo of a woman wearing sparkling earrings and a long sparkling gown, which are both sparkling even though it's a black and white photo. She's descending a staircase in a slight blur of motion. I walk up to it to see who the artist is in hopes that it would give me an idea of where I am. Then I realize that it's a painting. Done with a horsehair brush. Richter. That means nothing to me. But I like it, horsehair.

Heavy footsteps are coming up behind me and I turn to see three construction workers wearing those big canvas overalls. Carhartts or Dickies, I guess. The kind of cotton that would drag my frame to the floor.

Two of them lift the wall on my right. "You know what dees walls made of?" says one of the workers. "Balsa wood and plaster," he says without waiting for an answer. "Good tang. We be movin' dees tangs all the time," says the worker. Another rolls a dolly under the wall.

"Makes sense," I say.

"What? Rearrangin' dis museum all the time?"

"No. The balsa wood."

The workers shake their heads and frown at me. I'm reminded of the way I felt when I walked into a biker bar once in Ponchatoula, asked for a Stella and kept asking for more. That's a bad, true story.

"Wouldn't need balsa wood walls if dees walls were permanent. If dat curator make up his mind."

Unlike the balsa wood, the workers' accents make no sense to me. There's no way they talk like that in private.

Then they roll the wall around a corner, and I can hear the wheels on the dolly squeaking. It goes on for a while, like they're rolling it down a marbled tunnel, and then the echo fades and I lose it like the nightmare I might have had this morning.

I see the staircase to the curator's office behind where the wall had been and I start climbing up. I get to the top and see that his door is wide open so I walk in, real fast, trying to get up the courage to ask for a new assignment, but he's not there.

The laptop screen shines up on the wall behind the desk. "Hello?" a voice comes through the computer speakers. I go around the desk and see Nauman on the laptop screen. "Can you take your glasses off? There's a glare," Nauman says.

"Listen, I was just going to tell the curator I need a different exhibit. Don't take it personally." I rub my eyes and hang my glasses on my collar.

"But what's wrong with my exhibit?"

"I just can't stand there saying the same thing all day to every single person. It's too much. Or not enough."

"Just want to stare at Pointillism all day!" Nauman hacks more and the video feed gets all pixilated with his convulsing. He gets really pixilated. The word "Pointillism" gets corrupted by the slow transmission and Nauman is a mess of digital vocal hiccups.

"Yes. I want to stare at Pointillism all day."

"Listen. I never said to stop people from stepping on it. I just said don't put any distractions around it. Actually, you're doing exactly what I told you not to do. I wouldn't have required that the thing be installed in the floor if I gave a fuck if people would step on it."

"Then I don't need to be there."

"I don't follow. Just go back to the exhibit and don't open your mouth. I don't want you to do a damn thing. Even if someone pisses on it, just stand there and watch! The true artist helps the world by revealing mystic truths."

"That's some marvelous bullshit, Nauman."

When I get to the bottom of the stairs, I see all the way at the other end of the contemporary wing, one doorway, the only doorway in the entire wing now. The whole contemporary wing is one big lobby with one little exhibit in the corner. People wander around; some are crowding by the one doorway, which is blocked off by that velvet rope, others just walk until they meet the wall and turn back. Sam, standing by me, is leaning against the banister, peeling an orange, watching the people wander around.

"What happened to the other exhibits, Sam?"

"They ran out." He throws the orange peel to the ground.

"Ran out of what?"

"Not everybody lives on your timeline." He chomps down on the orange, wipes the juice from his mouth with his shirtsleeve. "Sorry. My blood sugar is low."

"I'm gonna get back to Nauman."

"Lots of people waiting to get in there. Him being so sick and all."

People are bumping into me and shoving me as I walk through the lobby; everybody is crowding around me following the same path, following me to the exhibit, stepping on each other's feet and knocking into my back. I'm trying to unhook the velvet rope to let people into the exhibit but everybody keeps pushing me so that I can't keep my hands steady enough.

Once I move the rope out of the way, the people flood in and I'm up against the wall. They're pushing and shoving each other all over the place, angry at the blank walls, stepping all over Nauman's Installation. And then the alarms sound and the red lights start flashing, and everybody, including me, covers their ears. I hug up against the wall even harder. The air smells of sweat and Chanel No. 5 and I walk over to the installation and see a piece of pink bubble gum stuck to it.

The alarms turn off and it's quiet until I hear footsteps and three construction workers come in and move a wall. Then more workers, and they move the next wall. They move every single wall, rolling them into a freight elevator one after the other, until there's nothing else in the entire contemporary wing except for me and what looks like a big bed in the opposite corner.

A neon light, mounted above a hospital bed, flickers and buzzes on, it reads *Artist In Residence*, with a flashing red arrow pointing down. I walk over and it starts smelling like a combination of chlorine and urine. Nauman is sleeping in the bed, machines beeping with his pulse, one bag to hydrate and one bag overflowing with his urine. He opens his eyes.

"I just wanted a little take and give," he says.

He spits some mucous into a towel resting on his chest. "All this is one endless salvage yard. I heard you: what happens after, weekends, a yard with a garden and maybe some of those orchids you can hang from a tree, that part I assumed, but home."

"I never brought any of that here."

"Just step on my installation. It won't answer. That's the matter of it." Nauman's head drops back to the pillow and the heart rate monitor sends out a steady high pitch. The workers start rolling walls back in so that I have to run towards my post at the installation, the walls locking into place behind me as I run.

("

The exhibit closes in together again and I'm standing there by myself, a bit nervous about what to do next. I'm bad at making decisions, especially in a place that lacks any consistency. I step on the installation, smearing the bubble gum with my shoes so that I cover up one of the HEREs. Sam walks into the room. He says, "They told me to tell you that you're fired."

Sam hugs me. And I hug Sam back, which surprises me a bit, but I like that I can't actually hug him too firmly because he's so fat. I get a sense that he'll never change.

"I'm sorry I gave you that map earlier," he says. "It was way off. I was way off."

"You were only trying to help." I pant a little into his collar, which is gross because his collar has a crease that's edged with that brown of sweat and dead skin.

I push him off, a little disgusted with my behavior.

"That's good," he says. "Here, I'll walk you out." He ushers me to the exit, which I don't remember having ever seen before.

GRANCY AND BAPOO ARE GOOD GRANDPARENTS

When Bapoo takes the elevator up to get dressed for dinner, the Mardi Gras beads jam the guide rails and he gets stuck in between the first and second floors. Vince, the oldest grandson, opens up the first floor door so that everybody can see Bapoo's feet as he sits on a small lounge chair. Vince then admits to Grancy that he had figured out a way to open the elevator's third floor door; he'd thrown a paper grocery bag full of beads down the shaft to see what would happen. All of the younger grandsons had watched him do it; they cheered.

Vince just wants to see what happens.

Grancy never likes to use the elevator; she likes to keep her legs toned. She doesn't like that Bapoo likes to use the elevator because he needs his exercise. Unfortunately, every townhouse in De Limon had come with an AmeriGlide Elite. It was not optional.

"You'll have to take dinner in the elevator tonight," Grancy says from the kitchen. She decides that accepting Bapoo's entrapment in an exaggerated manner is the best way to express her disapproval of Bapoo's using the elevator in the first place. Much like when he had volunteered for the Airforce right after telling Grancy that he loved her.

Grancy does not forget to add extra horseradish to the mashed potatoes on account of an old man named Tom Benson who expects his mashed potatoes a certain way, with extra horseradish. He had said he would come for dinner, maybe with his real pretty daughter. He lives a few houses down from Grancy and Bapoo. His house is huge and sometimes he lets everybody come over and play pool. The grandsons like to hide in Mr. Benson's garden and smoke his cigars; they started unbelievably young.

Vince thinks about Mr. Benson's real pretty daughter way too much. She's older than Vince. In fact she babysits the grandsons every once in a while. Vince doesn't have a chance with her. Unfortunately, Vince is convinced that true love, what he thinks he sees in the Sophia Loren movies, takes comedic timing to cultivate and is strengthened by emotional and physical uncertainties. He thinks he can wait for Mr. Benson's real pretty daughter to *come around*. In the meantime, Vince is content with her assuming that his clinging to her thighs is innocent.

Last year, Vince started rubbing his erection against his bed sheets because it felt good.

Grancy is like an American Sophia Loren. The grandsons know about Sophia Loren because Bapoo likes to watch Sophia Loren movies in the playroom while the grandsons beat each other up with pillows. He just puts the volume up real high. Grancy is like Sophia Loren because she's a redhead, tries to run the show, and also because she manages to age just as pretty. Once a neighborhood boy, Patrick, had come over to play and he told everybody that he thought Grancy was pretty. The grandsons all nodded, agreed with him, and later decided that Patrick couldn't come over anymore. She's *their* grandmother. The grandsons lied and said that Patrick used bad words, bullied the younger grandsons, and played with Bapoo's war medals. Patrick is not allowed over anymore.

Vince is hot so he decides that he won't be wearing his navy blue sport coat to dinner. The other grandsons are not hot but remain in their play clothes as well. Wearing play clothes to dinner thrills Vince. He points proudly at the exposed bruises and scabs that cover his brothers' knees and elbows. Grancy will not stop them from wearing play clothes to dinner, because she worries that they are still finding a way to grieve over the loss of their mom and dad. The loss of her son and daughter-in-law affects Grancy in small ways beyond her understanding, despite her age, and resulting experience, affording her larger understandings. She is not good at disciplining the grandsons and she knows it but she doesn't care. She doesn't know why she doesn't care.

You can see Bapoo's bruises and liver spots on his ankles as he sits inside the elevator, but unlike Vince, he is not proud of his bruises. "That's what happens when you get older," Bapoo says to the grandsons.

"It's gross," Vince says. "They're bruises, but they look nothing like our bruises."

Grancy walks up behind her grandsons. She is wearing a yellow sundress with lilies printed on it in faded shades of red and blue. "Fred, the boys are wearing their play clothes to dinner."

"From here all I can see are their feet. Why are they barefoot?" says Bapoo.

"They can't wear their dirty play shoes in the house," says Grancy.

"But their dirty play clothes?"

"Would you have them eat naked?" Grancy reaches into the elevator to give Bapoo a spoonful of pecan pie filling.

"Come on guys, let's go have a cocktail," Vince says to his younger brothers.

Vince and the rest of the grandsons don't realize it, but when Bapoo gives them liquor for their patio mini bar, he just fills his empty liquor bottles with water and adds food coloring. Bapoo is very good at falsifying the exact shades of Maker's Mark, Jim Beam, Johnny Walker, Glenfiddich, Herradura Gold, Mount Gay, Southern Comfort, Woodford Reserve, Sailor Jerry's, and some red wines. But the grandsons don't like red wine even though it tastes just like the Maker's Mark, Jim Beam, Johnny Walker, Glenfiddich, Herradura Gold, Mount Gay, Southern Comfort, Woodford Reserve and Sailor Jerry's. Since the grandsons don't know what alcohol tastes like, Bapoo has them convinced that all alcohol tastes like water. He knows that Vince will soon find out that alcohol doesn't taste like water, that it's actually more exciting than that, but he wants to stave off any kind of corruption in the boys' lives as long as possible. Grancy had said the whole thing was a bad idea.

Bapoo wonders if Vince is going through puberty because he recently started taking unusually long showers and laundering his own bed sheets almost every morning. It seems too early for that, Bapoo says often to himself, sometimes in the car, or shopping for groceries at the Sav-A-Center, or while putting the clean dishes back in the cupboard.

The first time Vince was really conscious of his cock, as more than something to just pee with, its sensitivity and the troubling control that it would have over him, was when he was baptized, a full submersion according to Baptist tradition. The water had been cold. And as he was lifted out of the water, Vince rubbed his eyes and slowly focused on what looked like a red wine cork pressing against his wet, white robe. After accepting Jesus Christ as his savior, Vince's prick, his balls, all felt tight, and for the first time he realized the depths of responsiveness his genitals had and will have. That night, at around ten, he masturbated for the first time. He would have done it earlier if his parents hadn't hosted a celebratory dinner welcoming Vince into the fold.

A few weeks later Vince's parents dropped him and his brothers off at Grancy and Bapoo's townhouse where the boys would stay while their parents traveled to Brasil on a missionary tour. After the parents collected their luggage and left the Dois de Julho International Airport in Salvador, their taxi blew a tire, lost control next to a logging truck.

Vince and his brothers don't attend Baptist church anymore. Grancy and Bapoo are Catholic.

"You're right, Peg," Bapoo says after he hears the patio door shut behind the grandsons. "It was a bad idea giving them a bar."

Vince lets his foot go numb, sitting cross-legged, stirring his Maker's Mark, wondering if Mr. Benson's real pretty daughter will come for dinner. If she doesn't, Vince promises himself that she will ruin him. Mr. Benson's daughter is somebody that is courted against her will on the black and white social pages of the Times-Picayune. She once asked Vince to paint her toenails, which he did with great care, but then she asked if she could paint his toenails, and he let her, she said that he had pretty toes, he thought hers looked better without paint, and then she said that she didn't have nail polish remover, so she walked Vince home, she walked him home, and he felt ridiculous because, wearing flip flops, his feet looked uncomfortably feminine with polish, and that can't be good for getting a girl like Mr. Benson's daughter. But he'd let her paint his nails again if he could.

He would never ask his grandparents if Mr. Benson's daughter will be joining them for dinner or going to a movie with Robbie, who, a sophomore at Tulane and point guard for their mediocre basketball team, would take her to the apartment that he shares with his Pi Kappa Alpha brothers and do things to her that Vince can't yet know or imagine if he himself may enjoy someday.

Vince slaps his foot hard against the brick patio, again and again. "Wake up." Then he leans forward, clutching his knees as the blood flows into his foot, and he feels the nerves throb with life. The other grandsons roll around on the patio, grinding wet moss into their cut-up britches, throwing their empty cups at each other, dumping the water from the liquor bottles over each other's heads, not cursing. "You know, brothers, that stuff isn't cheap. Bapoo and Grancy pay big bucks for the top-shelf sauce. Do something nice and go set the dinner table."

Grancy's arm is tired from whipping mashed potatoes. The electric beater is broken because the grandsons had tried to make a yellow cake for Vince's birthday just a few weeks ago. After Grancy and Bapoo made them clean the flour from the floor and pull the family silverware from the mangled beater, they took the grandsons to the Sav-A-Center to buy some Blue Bell mint chocolate chip ice cream and a microwavable cake kit. "Ice cream. I can't believe we got them ice cream after they ruined the beater," Grancy mumbles to herself. Then she convinces herself that it was okay because the grandsons had been trying to make a cake for their brother Vince and it was Vince's first birthday since the death of his parents.

"What were you saying, Peg?" Bapoo asks from the elevator, shuffling his feet.

"I'm afraid these mashed potatoes may be a little lumpy," says Grancy.

"Well, it's not worth wearing yourself out, Peg," says Bapoo. His feet cross each other. "I bet the bowl will fit through the opening. Let me work on the potatoes. I'm getting bored."

Grancy lifts the bowl and slides it onto the floor of the elevator and then licks the potatoes from her fingers. "They need more horseradish," she says. She returns and sticks her hand up into the elevator. "Here, Fred. Add a spoonful." She shakes the jar for Bapoo's attention.

"Kitchen appliances with child-proof locks," says Bapoo. "What an idea, huh, Peg?"

Grancy doesn't answer but sings "Chatanooga Choo Choo" as she fans the cornbread to make it get a strong, thin crust. And with what forearms he's got left, Bapoo whips the potatoes and peers through the opening of the elevator for a glimpse of Grancy's feet.

"I hate being stuck up here while you do all the work," says Bapoo.

Bapoo didn't hate being a pilot in the war but he hated being away from Grancy; he fell in love with her, went to training, and then ran off AWOL to marry her at that courthouse in Chattanooga. When he came back to the base, with a ring in his pocket but no honeymoon, the MPs let him through the gates and ignored recording anything in the log. As far as the Airforce knew, Grancy and Bapoo never got married. Bapoo's squadron passed him nudies, and he feigned excitement, waiting to write letters to Grancy every night in the dark.

The first mission in Bapoo's B-26, *Peg of My Heart*: the line in Marrakech was about to get thrown a bunch of supplies, mostly ammunition, to fight the German front in Africa, and right before the mission while everybody was strapping chutes to their asses, sweating on the navigation charts, Bapoo finally told the squad that he was married, and the whole squad cheered, took to the planes blessed with the stupid idea in their heads that no way a newly married squad leader would let them die.

The second mission: Aachen, and by then Bapoo had a

daughter. And the squad thought that no way would a new father let them die.

They were wrong to believe such idiotic things, but they all lived anyway. Except for the tail gunner.

Peg of My Heart was almost shot down when an antiaircraft shell hit the tail turret gunner, blew a hole where the tail gunner had been, and spat blood and Plexiglas shards into the filthy sky. All he heard through his headset was the crackle of the gunner disintegrating, and then he felt a hard jerk at the wheel, then screaming through his headset, the navigator yelling over the panics to tell the bombardier that they were over the target. And as the bombs dropped, Bapoo felt the pull on his wheel relent and he led the squad through evasive maneuvers that caused the big diesel engines to pop and gurgle so loud nobody could hear the exploding flak. Then it was quiet; they confirmed and reconfirmed that the gunner was dead, the air inside the plane feeling horribly refreshing as cool, wet winds came in through the hole. Before *Peg of My Heart* was repaired, somebody had to hose the blood from her tail—there was no body. Bapoo wrote a letter to the gunner's family and considered renaming his plane.

Grancy stayed in Chattanooga with her parents and the new baby. She began letters with "You must be somewhere in England" "You must be somewhere in Africa" "You must be somewhere in France" "You must be somewhere in Germany"— and because she runs the show, Grancy was always right—as if she predetermined everywhere Bapoo was sent to not die.

The doorbell chimes through the house and Grancy asks Vince to let Mr. Benson in. "Remember to shake his hand," says Bapoo. "And offer to take his hat," says Grancy. Vince washes his hands so that he can look at himself in the bathroom mirror.

He tries to make himself somebody that Mr. Benson's daughter could love. He rolls up his sleeves and admires the foundations of potential strength that hide somewhere in his undeveloped arms. He thinks the rolled-sleeve look is a good look. As he approaches the front door the stained glass windows keep him from determining if Mr. Benson's daughter came or not; then, struggling with the doorknob, losing his cool, Vince opens the door and displays his disappointment by not saying anything to Mr. Benson for a long time. It's not until Mr. Benson puts his hand out for Vince to shake that Vince remembers to ask for Mr. Benson's hat.

"Hello, Mr. Benson. May I take your hat?"

"I'm not wearing a hat, Vince."

Mr. Benson is an attractive man; a tall, broad man, he takes lumbering long strides instead of waddling ones, never gets a rash between his inner thighs. His suit pants don't make a swishing sound each time he walks into a hushed meeting.

"Actually Vince, I never wear hats." That's because Mr. Benson has a leonine head of blond hair that's reinforced by sideburns and a handlebar mustache and, with its indiscriminate appeal to enough women, was the cause of three marriages, three divorces, countless forgettable and unforgettable affairs, and one really pretty daughter.

Grancy comes down the hallway shaking her hands dry. "Hi Tom, how are you?" she says.

"You've met Grancy," Vince says to Mr. Benson. He gestures at her entrance with an open, outstretched hand.

"You mean Peg," says Mr. Benson.

"No. I mean Grancy," says Vince.

"Vince, stop playing with Mr. Benson." Grancy gives Mr. Benson a hug but Mr. Benson keeps hugging her after she tries to step away. "Come in, Tom. I'll have to make you a drink. Fred is stuck in the elevator."

"Stuck in the elevator?"

"Yes. And the repair man can't be here until nine tonight."

Grancy and Mr. Benson walk down the hallway, with Vince following slowly behind.

"Tom is here," says Grancy, and she continues into the kitchen.

"Fred. What the hell is going on?" says Mr. Benson.

"Tom, please," says Bapoo.

"Right." Mr. Benson, craning, trying to see Bapoo's face, reaches his hand out to search for Vince's head, pats Vince's head with his big hand, and smoothes the boy's hair down.

Vince fixes his hair by messing it up again.

"I got in here to go up and get ready for dinner. And then I heard this horrible crunching sound and the thing just stopped. Vince came clean and told me he threw some beads down the shaft from the third floor."

"Well don't you think we should call the fire department?"

"No, no. It's not an emergency. I don't want to cause a fuss."

"If it was me I would have called right away. A drink? Do you have a drink up there?"

"No."

"I swear I would have had a drink before I made the call. Of course, I don't really have anybody around to bring me a drink. Maybe I should keep a bottle in my elevator for emergencies. I'd need something for my nerves. Are you calm?"

Bapoo's feet do not move.

Grancy, excusing herself, pressing Vince and Mr. Benson up against the wall, walks back and forth between the kitchen and dinner table carrying serving dishes filled with things that smell of brown sugar, garlic, cayenne, cheese, and horseradish.

"Well, I'm bored actually," says Bapoo. "And I don't see how a drink could make staring at a wall any more fun."

"Never underestimate the power." Mr. Benson stops

suddenly as if he forgot what he was going to say.

After Bapoo does not respond, Mr. Benson laughs deep and loud and slaps the wall.

"Just some water would be nice," Bapoo says finally.

"Vince, go get your grandfather a glass of water."

Vince turns to the kitchen and Grancy nearly runs him over bringing a glass of water. "Here, Fred," she says and stands on her toes to reach into the elevator as much as she can.

Vince sees Mr. Benson looking at Grancy's legs, which, partly because she doesn't like the elevator, impress with well-proportioned calf muscles, some freckles, and thin ankles. Seeing Mr. Benson look at Grancy makes Vince feel a lot like how he felt when he saw Mr. Benson's daughter kissing her boyfriend on the couch.

"Vince dear, can you make your Bapoo a plate for me? Tom, I'll bring you a whiskey."

"Grancy, I want to make Mr. Benson's drink."

"No no, I'll do it. Just make Bapoo's plate for me."

After piling roast beef, mashed potatoes, shrimp, and bread pudding onto a plate, Vince reaches up, supporting the heavy plate with both hands, and offers the dinner to Bapoo who takes it, and thanks Vince for giving him extra gravy.

Mr. Benson moves his plate to where Bapoo's place setting had been and sits down next to Grancy.

Vince returns to the table and jerks out a chair, allowing the chair's legs to moan against the hardwood floors.

"Did you want to sit here, Vince?" Mr. Benson says.

"He's fine right there next to his brothers," Grancy says.

"Well, anyway I'm sorry my daughter couldn't make it. She's babysitting Patrick tonight. Patrick is a friend of yours, right Vince? Right boys?" Mr. Benson says.

"No," Vince answers.

"Oh, I thought he was."

"He's a bad kid."

"What he means is Patrick just doesn't have a lot in common with them," Grancy says.

"Peg, this is delicious," Mr. Benson chews and swallows a shrimp. "Fred, your Peg is an amazing cook," he yells, and then leaning over to Grancy and patting her arm, Mr. Benson whispers, "And a very beautiful cook."

At that the youngest grandson spits out his bread pudding with an audible squirt through tight puckered lips, sending out a flatulent-like noise of disapproval, inspiring a chorus of snickers from all the grandsons who then search for responses with volleyed gazes at Grancy and Mr. Benson.

"Mr. Benson, did you know that Bapoo has war medals?" Vince does not look up from the shrimp he is peeling.

"Yes, Vince. I've seen them."

"Do you have war medals, Mr. Benson?"

"No, Vince."

"Why not?"

"Because I was not drafted, because of a health concern."

"Do you feel bad about that, Mr. Benson?"

Grancy interrupts and tells Vince to be polite. Suddenly, she misses her son and daughter-in-law.

"No. It's okay," Mr. Benson says, patting Grancy on the forearm. "The boy is just curious. But no, Vince, I don't feel bad. I could not help my condition. I do feel bad for keeping so many women company though while the boys were off fighting. That, I feel somewhat guilty about."

"Tom, what an awful thing to say," says Grancy, shaking Mr. Benson's hand from her forearm.

"Oh, I'm just fooling. The boy has no idea what I mean, anyway."

"Grancy, I'm going to see if Bapoo wants seconds," Vince says and excuses himself from the table.

Vince learned the art of mockery when he watched Tommy Noonan in *Gentlemen Prefer Blondes*. Although he was turned off by the movie's title because he prefers women with darker hair and skin that reminds him of the color of sand in the evening, he watched the film with Bapoo and learned a little about people like Mr. Benson.

"Bapoo, I think Mr. Benson is flirting with Grancy," Vince whispers as he hands Bapoo another helping of shrimp.

"I'm sure he is," Bapoo answers.

"Well don't you think now is the time to call the fire department?"

"You think Mr. Benson's flirting with Grancy requires that I call the fire department?"

"You need the fire department to get you out of there so that you can watch out for Grancy."

"No I don't, son. Mr. Benson is a guest. And Grancy, and I, and you are his hosts and will show him hospitality."

"But Grancy - "

"Mr. Benson asked for a drink. And as much as y'all would like me to join you for dinner I cannot, so you will go and get him another whiskey. Besides, Grancy has never needed me or you to look out for her."

Vince glares at Bapoo's swelling feet, stomps off. He goes outside to the garden, to his patio mini bar, and pours Mr. Benson a Maker's Mark. He walks inside with the drink in hand and places it in front of Mr. Benson.

"Thank you, Vince." Grancy says.

Mr. Benson thanks Vince as he raises the drink to his lips. He drinks, drinks again, licks his lips and holds the drink up eye-level, shaking it, the ice cubes clinking against the crystal. Mr. Benson rubs his bushy, blonde mustache.

"Maybe it's watered down a bit?" Mr. Benson says.

"You see that tinge," Grancy says. "Looks like a strong pour to me, Tom."

"I see that. Maybe my taste buds are finally failing me." He takes another wide-mouthed taste, swallows.

The phone in the elevator, which is installed in every AmeriGlide Elite according to code, rings along with every other phone in the house. It wakes Bapoo from one of his sudden, shallow naps and he answers more out of shock than out of a genuine interest in who's calling. He clears his throat and then provides with various confirmations. He hangs the phone up. "Maggie is coming over," he says.

The doorbell chimes and Vince excuses himself. He wants to be the first to welcome Mr. Benson's real pretty daughter.

Maggie is nineteen years old and wearing tight white jeans made of a cotton, polyester, and spandex blend. Seventy percent cotton, twenty-eight percent polyester, and the two percent spandex that creates multiple definitions, which Vince doesn't yet understand. The green tank top she is wearing hangs loosely because it's her boyfriend's practice jersey, which she doesn't wear out of an intimation of intimacy. She puts a cigarette out in a pot of geraniums as Vince opens the door. She shoots up a stream of smoke into the damp night air and pats Vince on the head. Vince realizes this means that she doesn't take him seriously. He doesn't realize that it means she will never take him seriously.

"Hello, cutey," says Maggie.

"Maggie, I am not a puppy and I am not your cutey," says Vince. He thinks that this is playing hard-to-get and he thinks that this is how you get Maggie to take you seriously.

"Don't be a brat," says Maggie. She squeezes by Vince, through the door, grabbing his shoulders and turning him so she has the room. Vince is disappointed that the contact isn't intimate in some nature.

After taking her shoes off, Maggie slides down the hallway, her feet twisting and gliding against the soft wool of the oriental runner rug. She pulls a pencil from her back pocket and twists it into her tangled dark hair. Her bottom shimmies, shaking a black corduroy fanny pack that hangs from her hips.

As she rounds the corner, Vince hears his little brothers erupt with laughter and screams, welcoming Maggie. Vince sees her bottom again when it pokes around the corner as Maggie bows heroically for the younger grandsons. When Vince returns to the dining room, Maggie is still bowing. "Thank you, my adorable little misfits," she says.

"I will get you another drink," Maggie says. She grabs her father's glass and walks to the liquor cabinet.

"Let me do it. Please, Maggie." Vince doesn't remember the last time he begged for anything. "Please. You can help," he says.

Grancy is rubbing her forehead explaining to the younger grandsons again why they can't have a dog. "Your Grancy is too old to help you boys care for a dog. I'm too old to…Vince, leave Maggie alone please."

"But she's helping me get Mr. Benson another drink." Vince holds Maggie's hand and walks her outside to his patio mini-bar. "I'll even pour him the black Walker." He slams the door shut.

Empty bottles, wet with the mud and moss that creeps through the brick, cover the patio. Moths swarm and glow green and orange against the floodlight. Maggie lights a cigarette. "It's like a frat house out here," she says.

Vince digs a glass through the mini-fridge for ice cubes. "Yes, there are a lot of us."

"Vince, listen. I don't think my dad wants that kind of drink."

"Gin?"

"I don't mean to shatter your world here, kid, but none of that stuff is real. It's just water. Trust me, I raided this thing a long time ago after y'all had gone to bed."

Vince previously had assumed that when he went to bed Maggie also went to bed, until he had gone downstairs one night to find her on the couch, kissing her boyfriend Robbie. As Vince watched Robbie move a hand up Maggie's shirt, he felt very pathetic for all those times he had wrapped his arms around Maggie's thighs under the guise of innocence.

"People drink to get drunk, mostly," says Maggie. Her cigarette smoke gets stuck in the humidity and Vince begins to feel nauseous.

Maggie slides her black corduroy fanny pack around, the straps leaving little red marks on her hipbones, and she pulls out a silver flask. "Here, kid, try this." She raises the whiskey to Vince's lips. "Drink."

Vince coughs, spitting the whiskey on Maggie's feet, which have a clear acrylic overlay and blue French tips.

"So that's what your black Walker is supposed to taste like." She turns and goes back inside, leaving the door open behind her. "Vince is out of booze!" she announces to everybody as she makes her way to the kitchen to find Bapoo's liquor cabinet. The grandsons *boo* with disapproval.

As dinner concludes, and the grandsons, all except for Vince, go up to the playroom to beat on each other with pillows, and Grancy serves the praline pie, and Bapoo, still stuck in the elevator, snores, and Maggie yawns having only eaten the dinner rolls, Mr. Benson says *no* to another drink and wipes his mouth on the linen napkins.

Maggie dips her unused and still neatly folded napkin

into her glass of ice water. She props her feet up on Vince's insufficiently sized lap and throws the damp napkin at him. "Clean that whiskey off my pedicure."

Vince asks Grancy if he may see Mr. Benson and Maggie to the door.

On the oyster shell driveway: The suffocating air combined with Mr. Benson's dropping blood alcohol level makes the old man sweat. He takes a deep breath and wipes his brow as he walks down the bed of chalky oyster shells, holding Maggie's arm to steady himself.

Maggie unzips her fanny pack and pulls out her cigarettes. With one hand opening the pack and the other steadying her father, Maggie flicks the pack so that a cigarette pops into her lips. She kisses the filter and pulls the cigarette out, returns the smokes to her fanny pack and pulls out her lighter.

"Your dad knows you smoke?" Vince asks.

"I don't like to rub it in his face, but I was getting a little antsy." The glow from the cigarette dances up and down as Maggie mumbles against the filter in between her lips.

"I hate your smoking, love," Mr Benson says.

Maggie reaches in her fanny pack and pulls out her flask. She takes a sip and then puts it to her father's lips. He drinks.

"I'm not thrilled about the drinking either," he says.

Vince stops at the end of the driveway and Mr. Benson and Maggie turn to him. The sky is low like a giant blue and gold circus tent slowly collapsing, billowing against the air that's trapped inside of it. "What about the boys?" Vince says.

"What about them?" Mr. Benson says.

Maggie lets out a laugh muffled with a small cough. She smiles and shakes her head.

"Robbie was over the other night. They were kissing on our couch," Vince says.

"You probably should have been asleep," Mr. Benson says.

Vince feels that the circus tent, now a dark blue, threatens to suffocate him. He feels that, despite the sky still billowing safe above in the wind and smoke.

Then Maggie bends over and kisses Vince on the forehead. "You're gonna need a better sense of humor." Then she shakes her dad's arm. "I think Vince is getting too old for a babysitter. Right, Dad?"

"Yes, probably unavoidable." He closes his eyes and nods in apology.

"All those boys. Man, I feel for Grancy," Maggie says as she turns with her dad and walks away.

Her two percent spandex definitions, even brighter white against the unlit street and sleeping townhouses, still confuse Vince.

Upon entering Vince's bedroom to kiss his grandson goodnight, the recently liberated Bapoo notices that Vince is asleep but madly clutching his pillow. Bapoo turns the light out and leaves the room. "Poor boy," Bapoo says as he lumbers down the hallway to get in bed with Grancy. He wonders if the night would've ended differently if he had not been stuck in the elevator. Then, he laughs at himself, feeling the fool for thinking he could have such consequence. The soft bristle of the elevator carpeting against his bare feet reenters his thoughts, and he hopes that it won't be death that teaches the grandsons how to live.

Maggie would refuse to babysit the grandsons ever again.

SUNDAY BRUNCH WITH DAISY

"You know how to make scrambled eggs, don't you?" she said, smiling at me from under my new, white sheet. Spilling over my pillowcase, her curly red hair framed her green eyes, puffy and lined with sleep. We'd gone out for breakfast the past three mornings. We hadn't had sex, just slept together. We slept naked and did nothing, really. That was hard. I shrugged it off and threw on some pants and a flannel shirt, still seeing green on white with every waking blink. Her eyes — and my confusion — led me to the kitchen where I yelled to her, "Do you like cheese?"

"Oh, it doesn't matter. Just hurry up and come back to bed," she said quickly.

In my kitchen, I found the skillet already on the stove from a grilled cheese I'd made for dinner the night before. I cracked four eggs into a flesh-toned ceramic bowl. The frustration from the past three nights made me whip the eggs a little harder than I needed.

I turned a knob on the stove. The starter kept cracking, the gas wouldn't catch; I smelled the gas until it caught and threw up flames like an orange and blue daisy bloom, thundering and fluttering. I poured the eggs on the skillet. My belly started feeling hot from the flames.

"It's ready!" I yelled and threw some shredded cheddar and Chachere's on top of the eggs.

I turned to make my way back to the bedroom.

But there she stood wrapped in my sheet, pointing my gun at me. I looked at the gun, and behind it, her green eyes squinted on my forehead.

"Hand 'em over!" she said with a bad smile.

"What the fuck you think you're doing!" I yelled, snatching the glock away from her and checking the safety.

"Oh relax!" she laughed and grabbed some grapefruit juice from my fridge.

"Where'd you get this!" I said, quickly putting the gun on the counter and stepping away.

"By your bed. The nightstand."

"Yeah, I know!" I said. I was glaring at her.

"So?" she laughed.

"So, get out of my house!" I yelled.

She threw the cup of juice into the sink.

"It's just, where do you get off looking through my shit?" I said.

"Where do you get off yelling at me?" She took a bite of the eggs and chewed on them slowly. "God, they're salty," she said and spit them in the sink. She grabbed her purse from the coffee table and walked right out the door, with my bed sheet still wrapped around her.

It was a quarter after nine in the morning and I walked out to my stoop with my skillet of eggs. "That's a nice sheet!" I yelled at her as she got in her car. "Hey, that's Egyptian cotton!"

Across the street, early Mass was letting out of Saint Augustine. The whole flock was staring at me, having just seen a naked woman run through the street with my linens. I gave a little wave. "Morning ya'll," I said.

I sat down, trying to figure out why she didn't just get dressed instead of taking my sheet. Why had I bought that gun?

I put the eggs down and grabbed my tobacco pouch. Ronald, my neighbor across the street, stormed through his screen door. The spring coil whipped his door back to the wood frame; the smack made every dog on the block bark. Still dressed in his painting coveralls, Ronald paced back and forth in the five-square-foot lawn that sat between his porch and his metal fencing. I heard yelling coming from his house, but all the dog barking made it impossible to understand. Ronald pulled out a white handkerchief from his back pocket and wiped off his forehead as he leaned against his fence. I rested my chin on the knuckles of my hands and watched.

The sunlight shined on Ronald's bald black head as he perched his tall body against the fence. His thin fingers rubbed back and forth over his scalp.

The dogs stopped barking and I heard his wife cry from inside the house. The voice sounded angry and desperate.

"Ronald, goddamn it!" she yelled in a deep hollow gurgle. "You better get in here!" whimpering as she said the last few words.

I looked at him until he turned and saw me on my stoop. I picked up the eggs and tried to ignore him, but he started toward me, then stopped and lifted up his left shoe with a scowl on his face. Looking at the bottom of his shoe and scowling more, he stomped his foot down, kicking and wiping it against the cracked pavement while he crossed the street.

Ronald swung my wrought-iron gate out of his way and with one long-legged step he reached my porch. He hoisted his left leg up onto my third step and leaned on his knee. I stared at the shoe resting next to me and my skillet of eggs. The smell of dog shit stole my appetite.

"My old lady's sick of Daisy," he said and quickly looked back over each side of his shoulders. "Took her to a vet last Friday," he continued. "It's too much. The surgery." He looked down at the eggs. "What eggs that is!" he laughed at me.

"Just scrambled. Try them."

Ronald picked up the skillet and scooped a bite into his mouth.

"Damn, that's salty! You got a beer?" he said.

"In the fridge," I said, and grabbed back the skillet. "Wait, I'll get it for you. Just let me smoke this," I lifted my empty cigarette paper towards him.

Ronald looked over his shoulders again.

"So what?" I asked.

"Give me your gun," he said. He tried giving me a friendly smile.

"Man, you're crazy. I don't have a gun," I said.

"That vet bastard wants me to pay a hundred dollars to put Daisy out."

"Hundred dollars!" I yelled. "That doesn't sound right."

"Yeah, well she's a big dog. At least hundred-ten pounds."

I kept staring at Ronald, waiting for him to continue.

"And I ain't paying that. Just let me borrow it."

"What, you just gonna shoot it in your backyard."

"I'll try."

"There's got to be some law against that."

"Yeah, sure," he said as he picked some jasmine flowers from the side of my house.

"How the hell do you know about my gun?" I asked.

"Saw it during the Labor Day barbecue. I was using your commode and saw it sticking out from under your pillow… when I walked through your bedroom," he explained slowly, putting the jasmine up to his nose.

"Gun's registered under my name."

"Why was it under your pillow?" Ronald asked.

"I don't know, but the gun's…" I tried to say before stopping myself to wonder why the gun was under my pillow.

"I'll bring it right back," he urged. "She's in a lot of pain, man! And my old lady's getting' sick of hearin' her moan all night. Dog's moanin', old lady's yellin' at me, I think I'm gonna pop both of'em."

"All right, all right. Don't tell anybody where you got it, okay?" I said. Ronald nodded. "And try to muffle the shot with a blanket or pillow or something."

"I know. Just like in the movies, right?" Ronald said.

"It smells like shit." I huffed and got up to go inside. I walked in and shut the door behind me, leaving Ronald outside. I grabbed the gun from the counter and put it in an old Nike gym bag on my floor. There were some black socks stinking in the bag. I left them in there with the gun.

I went back outside and handed the bag to Ronald immediately. He lifted it eye level and bit down on his bottom lip.

"You're a fuckin' nut," I said, shaking my head. "It's already loaded. There's one in the chamber. Just turn the safety off, pull the trigger, kill her and bring it back."

Ronald rocked back onto his right leg, almost raising his eyebrows to the top of his shiny head. He pulled his handkerchief from his back pocket and swept his brow and chin for sweat.

"You think maybe you could help me?" he asked.

"For about a hundred dollars," I said.

Another cry came from his house. It sounded more like a roar this time, yelling Ronald and some profanity.

"I'm sick of the old bitch," Ronald said and lifted the gym bag a little to feel its weight before turning back towards his house. I stared at the bag its whole trip to Ronald's house, until the screen door slapped back against the doorframe again, causing another chorus of barking.

Only a few minutes and he'll be bringing it back, I thought. I grabbed some tobacco and pressed it into the crease of my paper. The paper crackled and wrinkled as I started rolling the tobacco back and forth to tighten it. I finished rolling the cigarette and put it between my lips. I lit my cigarette. I decided to wash off the dog shit Ronald had left on my stoop and grabbed my neighbor's hose. I turned the water on but the pressure was too high and dog shit started spitting every which way off my steps; the smell intensified. I'd almost gotten all the shit off when a loud thud shot down the street like a sledgehammer slamming down on pavement. The shock made me drop my cigarette; it let out a long sizzle when it hit the water.

Ronald came running out pushing his screen door open again. The same smack from the door caused me to jump and the dogs to bark. He had the gym bag, but Daisy was hanging from his other arm. A brown bloodhound with its big goofy ears flopping all around and blood dripping from its mouth in thick dark streams all coming towards me and my house; the biggest bloodhound I'd ever seen. Ronald kicked my wrought-iron gate out of his way, struggling with the dog, and gave me the Nike bag. I threw the bag inside and slammed my front door shut.

"Ron!" I yelled, leaning myself against my front door, looking for sturdy ground. "What the hell are you doing?"

Ronald's face was wrinkled up with tears and crying. I noticed a similarity between the expression on his face and the dog's chubby wrinkled face. I coughed up a laugh. "Ron, is the thing dead?"

"Naw, man!" he cried. "I don't think she is! I fucked up! I pulled back at the last minute!"

Some drops of Daisy's blood glistened on Ronald's face. Then the dog's eyes looked to me and expressed a need for answers. I felt sick.

"I think I got her in the back of the neck!" Ronald cried. "Please, man. You got to do it! I can't! I fuckin' can't. I've never killed a dog before!"

"You think I have? I'm not gonna sacrifice the thing on my

steps. That's a big animal!"

Across the street, Ronald's fat wife charged through her front door, her huge breasts working as battering rams. She looked up and down the street.

"Bring the fucking thing inside," I said and opened my door.

Ronald hunched through my door, cradling the dog.

"Watch the carpet!" I yelled.

"Okay, okay," he said and started pacing back and forth in my kitchen.

"Put her in the laundry room. I'm gonna lose my deposit over this," I said, looking at the blood trail on the carpet.

I grabbed the gun and threw the bag back on the floor as I stomped towards the laundry room. I picked up an old dirty pillow sitting next to my couch. It was thick and hard. I figured it would work well. Ronald left the laundry room and ran past me.

"I'm gonna wash my hands," he said.

"We're not finished yet!" I yelled, but Ronald ignored me.

I went through the laundry room doorway and saw the dog on the floor. Blood was running to the floor drain. It was the first time anything had ever gone down that drain. The dog's eyes looked tired and confused as her thick lids clumped to a close and then opened again. She was breathing slowly but smoothly. I put the tip of the gun in front of her ear and then pulled the gun straight back. Her eyes, swollen with fear and anticipation, followed the gun's moves. She knew the gun's business now; before Ronald shot her she didn't know a thing about guns, but now, her eyes closed as I placed the pillow down on her head. I pressed the gun back down, this time on the pillow. I took a deep breath, exhaled slowly and lifted the pillow back up. I placed the gun down in front of her wet nose. She lay there with her eyes closed tightly.

She slowly opened her eyes again and looked at the gun.

She sneezed, spraying some blood onto the black barrel. The drain couldn't keep up with all the blood that she was pumping out her neck.

I watched her eyes and then placed the pillow over her head, concentrating all of my weight over her nose. I held my weight right over her nose, feeling her jaw pressing through the pillow. I sat still, trying not to count, until I felt a heavy paw push against my left ankle and then let back.

Ronald came back into the laundry room and crouched behind the dog, biting down on his knuckles. I rocked back onto my butt. We both stared at her. She wasn't breathing anymore and the blood had pooled around us. I left the pillow on top of Daisy's head.

"You didn't use the gun?" Ronald asked quietly, trying not to cry.

"Didn't need to," I said, turning my attention to my slow floor drain.

Ronald jerked his head up from his gaze on Daisy, peering over me at something.

"I know you," Ronald said cheerfully, wiping his tears from his face and forcing a smile. "I saw you yesterday morning. You was leaving this house."

I turned around and those green eyes were staring back, but not at me, at the dog.

"So this is why you have the gun," she said.

She looked good, wearing a white tank top with some cutoff khakis and holding my bed sheet in one hand. Her curly red hair was loosely tied back, some hanging down over her right cheek. Her toes looked clean and slender, gripping her black flip-flops. My bed sheet, smooth and clean, ran down the length of the girl's thigh and calf. I couldn't think of anything to say, still trying to recover myself.

Then she threw my bed sheet on the bloodied floor. Daisy's

blood ran its course through the white stitching. I got up, slipping on the wet linoleum and falling back on my ass. My shoes squeaked as they rubbed against the bloody floor for traction.

"No! That's Egyptian cotton!" I yelled, but it was too late for the sheet. The girl turned and started for the door. "Wait! I didn't—Ronald just needed some help!"

"Just an accomplice, huh? You're messed up, man"

Man, I hated hearing that. Man, she said it as if she was already trying to forget my name.

Gritting my teeth in search of the last word, I stood at my front door and watched her walk to her car.

"All right, Ronald!" I yelled, staring at her as she got in her car. "I'll get the mop!" I yelled, but she was gone.

I turned back around. Ronald was standing by my kitchen counter, holding the skillet and eating the last of the eggs. He had missed a spot of blood above his right eyebrow. I turned and gazed out my door at the car driving away. "You got dog on your forehead," I said.

Ronald dropped the skillet and pulled out his handkerchief. "What's the big deal with Egyptian cotton anyway?" he asked, wiping away the blood and a few more tears.

THE BOOT

It was even hotter when I walked inside the Army Surplus Store. A brass bell rang as the door slammed shut behind me. In the far left corner there was a big black furnace with flames glowing inside. I started sweating out last night's NyQuil. I took off my fleece and I smelled canvas and the air felt heavy in my nose. My footsteps felt soft and unsteady on the sawdust and sand that covered the floor.

All the shelves were empty. And the garment racks stood bare. There wasn't any merchandise in the store except for a tattered boot that sat on the floor near the store entrance. It was definitely a desert boot, but in real bad shape. No laces, a big hole in the toe, half the sole missing, and some brown stains.

I was about to turn and walk out, shrug it off as closed, until an old man yelled at me as he came out from behind a thick green blanket fashioned as a curtain.

He stood behind the counter with a brass National cash register. Wearing a thin but dark flannel and round-framed black glasses, he almost blended into the curtain. "Hello. Hello," he said. "Please, can I help you?"

I walked towards him a little bit to get a closer look, still feeling as if I could slip on the sawdust. He had an uneven shave and a tarnished but beautiful silver cross hanging from his neck.

"I was just looking for a tent," I said. "I'm going camping."

He bent down behind the counter, showing me the bony small of his back and a dry, cracked leather belt on blue jeans. "Let me see," he said, and came back up with a large brown leather-bound book filled with thick sheets of yellow paper,

"Inventory" labeled on its cover. A blue silk ribbon dangled from the top of the binding.

"Doesn't look like you got much of anything," I said to the old man and immediately felt guilty.

"Now just hold on, son," he said, waving a hand back and forth. "You said you wanna go camping so let me see what I can do for you."

I approached the counter. I could see his feet. He was wearing some of those thick foam sandals, like the kind you could buy at the drug store.

"If you're gonna go camping you're gonna need more than just a tent," the old man started. "You're gonna be thirsty so you need a canteen." He flipped through several pages of the book. "Beebee gun, Buck knife. Here, Canteen." He scanned the page, moving his head back and forth. "No." He shook his head.

I laughed a little bit thinking he was joking with me.

"Well," he continued, flipping through the book again. "You're also gonna need a mess kit." He flipped back and forth between two pages, picking one and again scanning the page back and forth. "No."

"Fresh out?" I said. "Listen, sir. I just wanted a tent and I doubt you have one so I'm just gonna go."

"Ah, yes," he said and started flipping through the book again.

"Why don't you just give me your number?" I saw an old rotary phone hanging on the wall. A fan behind the counter made the unplugged phone jack sway slowly back and forth. "I'll call you later about the tent," I mumbled.

Just then, the bell rang from the front door, a lot louder than I had remembered. The old man looked around me and he put his head down.

I turned and saw a little man, hunched over, draped in a

peacoat that swallowed his shoulders and went down below his knees. He didn't acknowledge us at all. He just walked over to the old desert boot, grabbed it and walked slowly across the store to us. He sort of sauntered. He stopped behind me and I turned to look at him. His arms hung down but extended forward a little bit, like he was ready to draw pistols. I kept staring at him, wondering why he had stopped behind me.

"Oh, sorry," he said with an embarrassed smirk and tight, thin lips. "Thought you good folks were doing business." He reached around me and threw a bill on the counter. "Just the boot, Mr. Pat."

I looked at the bill. It was a hundred, and that made no sense to me.

"But that's my last one, Sir," the old man said.

"The boot, Pat." The little man shouldered me out of his way and placed his hands on the counter.

"I'll have nothing left." The old man was begging now. He reached for the little man's left hand and held it with both of his. "Nothing," he cried.

"Just let the old man keep his boot, man," I said.

The little man looked at me and his eyes were a soft blue and his skin tanned with just a few wrinkles on his forehead and I swear I saw a bit of me in those eyes and I was scared of him. Then he jerked his hand away from the old man and I heard a bang.

I was on my ass, my hands reaching behind me to push myself back up on my feet. There was a burnt smell in the air and a gurgling sound, followed by a choked coughing. I crawled around the counter and found the old man on his back, holding his throat. The blood was coming out his neck and through his fingers as if he was squeezing a paint sponge. I screamed something and tried to crawl towards him but my knees and hands slipped on his blood.

I tried ripping that blanket from the curtain rod but the material was too thick. I screamed something else that I don't recall and then I started apologizing, looking around us for anything to stop the bleeding as I propped his head up in my lap. I grabbed the inventory book and started ripping pages from it. The old man's bloody hands grabbed my arms and pulled them away from the book. His blood pumped freely and his eyes were big and he was shaking his head.

As the bleeding came to a steady trickle, the old man was blinking his eyes slower and slower and with one hand he reached for my shoulder as if to try and stand, and with his other hand he pointed at the whispering furnace.

TIME OF DELIVERY

At nine in the morning you write in your daily planner that after you convince the judge to drop your Section 10-125 by ten, you'll have enough time to take the N to 42nd Street and get a coffee before your job interview with *The New Yorker* at eleven. While in commute, you'll study a printout of recent articles from the magazine in preparation for your interview. You write with a medium, black crystal stick *BiC* that you'll get a small medium roast coffee, and then only drink one-third of it, before throwing it into a trashcan where maybe it will collide with some other piece of refuse and splash back up and towards you. The splash of coffee will land on one of your calfskin shoes, you determine, but you know the problem will fix itself, because by the time you enter the Conde Nast building at 4 Times Square and let the elevator deliver you to the 20th floor, the coffee will have dried on the leather and, besides a slight color incongruence, for the most part be inconspicuous. It is a plan. And you can sacrifice the color consistency of a shoe for the plan if you have to.

In case of any inconsistencies, you leave your planner open, resting on your thigh, ready for even the most minor amendment while you sit among other misdemeanor offenders in Courtroom 3 at the New York City Criminal Courthouse.

The courtroom is reminiscent of a public schoolroom. White linoleum floors meet blue ceramic tile walls, as if the courtroom's only design is based on a convenience for cleaning. After all us criminals receive our sentences, you write, and go home or back to jail, a large man covered from head to toe in a rubber suit will come into this courtroom and spray all the filth to hell with a giant pressure washer at exactly eleven tonight.

The noise from the pressure washer will be deafening, but the tile and linoleum will shine. And the court will convene the next morning as if for the first time.

In what looks like a temporary arrangement turned permanent, rows of wooden pews face a judge's bench made of particleboard and vinyl. You sit in this arrangement, observing the men, and they are all men, who sit with you waiting for names to be pronounced incorrectly.

In civilized public buildings, public servants communicate through signed documents and carbon copies of signed documents, summoning names and dispensing terms of existence. You sit in amazement of the automatism behind every decision by the judge and her staff. Refusing to make eye contact with the subjects of the documents or even their fellow coworkers, they shuffle these decisive terms with the ease of a dealer at a hold'em table, and their dull expressions remind you of those you've paid at tollbooths.

Despite the court system's efforts to maintain order, you take into account that even though your summons indicates a 9 AM hearing for your charge, it will most likely be held around ten. You admire the stenographer, if not for her determination, for allowing her unkempt black hair to keep asserting itself over her shoulder and into the machine's keys. Despite her efforts to record the events of the day, her work will not be admitted in future proceedings, but thrown out for lack of relevance.

Your crime is minor but still a crime according to a numbered law, and there is a vague sense of guilt, and it makes you stare into one of the crud linoleum and tile corners of the courtroom, where you imprison yourself to beg forgiveness for your actions the other night and other nights. It isn't just dust and moisture from dirty shoe soles in that corner. You hope the corner serves as a landfill where you'll leave your guilt, and that as soon as the judge dismisses the charge, your guilt will be exiled to that corner where it will rot until the man in the rubber body suit comes and washes it away with one thousand electric-powered PSIs of water and bleach.

A clerk, a curvy and provocatively dressed clerk, belches your name up as if she blames you for the indigestion that she suffers from the sausage biscuit she ate that morning. You stand.

Until then you've had no real sense of the impending penitence that would be dispensed by the Honorable Gloria Lilley. Until then, you have not been nervous. But as you 'approach the bench,' the reality of your situation makes your heart beat almost audibly, and the fine print, which denotes the maximum sentence for your offense, somehow becomes an actual possibility. Three Days in Jail and up to a $125 Fine.

This is all so unlike you, you hear your mother say. You're lucky they didn't rough you up, talking how you were. You know how bourgeois and childish you sound, telling officers they should be locking up drug dealers instead of wasting time with a casual drunk.

Sometimes you do drink too much, casually. And who are you to tell anybody how to do his or her job? You feel bad about that one. It isn't the being drunk or walking around with a twenty-four-ounce can of Tecate that summons what guilt you feel.

As the judge shuffles papers in order to distinguish your presence in her court, you refer to your planner quickly and remind yourself that this is when the judge would say, *Obviously, your poor behavior the other night was just a slip up. I'm going to dismiss the charge. You're free to go. And, for the record, you are definitely New Yorker material. You're hired, by the power vested in me...*

"You're accused of violating Section 10-125 2b of the New York City Administrative Code on Sept. 1, 2009. How do you plead?" Signing documents, the judge does not look up from her desk. She does not look at you or admire your appearance.

"Your honor, I realize what I did was wrong, but, in my defense, I just moved here from a city where they don't have open container laws," you say, a bit too eager.

The judge interrupts you. "You either plead guilty or not guilty," she says. "If you plead not guilty we schedule another hearing where you then make your defense and confront testimony by the arresting officer."

"I understand, ma'am, but I am really…

"Please don't waste my time telling me something just because you think I want to hear it."

"Guilty, your honor," you say, telling Judge Lilley exactly what she wants to hear.

"Fine is twenty dollars."

Your unsteady knees suddenly turn sluggish. The clerk hands you the plea agreement and points you in the direction of a window where you can pay your fine with Visa. On the upside, it seems efficient that you would only once go through the trouble of dressing nice for two separate and semi-formal events. Although it was a coincidence, you feel you accomplished something and you experience a sense of satisfaction.

LADIES AND GENTLEMEN, WE ARE BEING HELD MOMENTARILY BY THE TRAIN DISPATCHER. PLEASE BE PATIENT.

The N train holds you in your tenth minute of arrest, stuck in the vein that connects 34th Street to 42nd Street. You've heard the computer-generated voice attempt to calm your nerves exactly three times already in those last ten minutes. You look at your planner and try to discern the numerical significance of "momentarily." Nothing from your printout of *New Yorker* material takes hold, and after furiously rereading the first page, you gaze outside the train's windows—the tunnel innards vibrate with the traffic above and have a color and texture that resembles the corners of the courtroom.

Across from you, a new version of Bemelmans' *Madeline* is being performed among the orange and cream-colored seats and consists of two black women enveloping the small hands and minds of twelve white children wearing pea coats of fashionably and seasonally conscious bright colors—red, yellow, and blue.

The children yell about kissing boys or not kissing girls, the nannies tell them to hold onto the railings, they all agree on hot chocolate by the ice rink. And then the transit system's computer-generated representative comes again with, *LADIES AND GENTLEMEN…*

"WE ARE BEING HELD MOMENTARILY BY THE TRAIN DISPATCHER!" scream the *Madeline* children in unison. "PLEASE BE PATIENT!"

The two nannies laugh and reward the children with hugs and kisses. In an effort to ward off any further assault on your senses from the screaming children, or the stench from last night's vomit that percolates through the train's heating apparatus, you pull out your iPhone and plug your ears. The battery is dead. And the *New Yorker* material ends up on the train floor with the babies' discarded Barnum's Animal Crackers.

"When will we get hot chocolate?" one of the little girls says in a charming whine.

"When we get there, silly love," the nanny responds.

"If we ever get there," you blurt out at the lit screen tracking the train's progression through its route. "These screens are pointless. They have no concept of time."

A little boy walks over to you, wiping his nose with the blue sleeve of his pea coat. He looks at you and then at the lit route screen above the train window. "Are you late for something?" Snot dries into an adorable crust below the boy's nostrils.

"I might be," you answer quietly.

"You sound like my dad."

"How old is your dad?"

"How should I know?" Pepito says.

And you feel a little foolish because, of course, why would Pepito know how old his dad is.

"Pepito, get your behind back here!" a nanny yells at the boy.

The boy turns and walks back to the troop of children.

"Pepito, at this rate, I won't get my coffee and you and your friends aren't gonna get your hot chocolate," you say.

With this comment comes a chorus of whines from all the children. One of the nannies immediately stands up and corrals the children, moving them to the other end of the train car. The other nanny tugs down at her sweater as she stands up and walks toward you, staring at you with sure and angry eyes.

"Listen to me," says the nanny. "You don't mess with my kids."

The N train begins moving again towards 42nd Street, gradually picking up speed. Just as a sense of calm tries to come over you, the nanny grabs onto the overhead railing above you so that her large breasts loom ominously over your face and threaten to knock you with each jerk the train makes on the inconsistent track. An unquestionable sense of authority travels in the scent wafting from the wool of her sweater.

"You understand me?"

"Yes ma'am. I'm sorry," you say and tilt your head back.

You haven't been able to get a small cup of coffee but you did arrive five minutes early for the interview, providing just enough time to dwell on your lack of preparation and work yourself into a comfortable degree of paranoia as you look at a scattering of the publication's recent issues on the lobby table and fail to recognize a single one. The best way to handle this kind of opportunity is to pretend it's not a big deal, you tell yourself.

The secretary points to the left, her red polished nails vulgar against the tan slab of drywall constructed behind her for the office's privacy. You follow the drywall, its artless drapery ushering you into what looks more like a drab accounting office than an institution of culture. Amidst the monochromatic wall-to-wall carpeting and vinyl-covered cubicles stands a young man in fitting jeans and a buttoned cardigan over a t-shirt.

"Please take a seat," he says, removing his eyeglasses. He motions towards a conference room furnished with a bare wooden table and black-cushioned office chairs. "I'm glad you could schedule a meeting on such short notice."

"It only required some minor adjustments," you say.

The editor pauses for a moment and smiles expectantly at you, before taking his seat and setting it to the highest sitting.

"Yes. Well, we liked what you had to say in the two reviews. First of all, though, I'm a bit confused about your present job. Could you explain it to me?"

"I write movie synopses for the NETFLIX online data bank. Unfortunately, the number of movies I have to summarize is so overwhelming that I can't actually watch any of the movies I write about. So I read the industry treatments, and pull out the necessary details from those in order to summarize the movies."

"That's definitely an explanation."

"I just figured I'd satisfy the question as much as possible."

"That's appreciated. So you don't actually watch any movies?"

"No."

"But you know the ending of every movie you've never seen?"

"In a way. The ones I've written about at least," you respond a little too enthusiastically.

"Honestly, that seems a little frustrating. Definitely unsatisfying."

"Well, working from home can be nice. I do things on my own schedule."

"Yes, but you couldn't do that here."

"I like to think I could adapt."

"So what have you read in *The New Yorker* lately that you liked, what stuck out in your mind?"

You're sure you've read something from the magazine that interested you, at one time, but now you can't remember one article, in fact, it's as if you've never read the magazine.

The editor stops rocking back in his chair. He sits up slowly and rests his elbows on the conference table, pulling your resume out of a folder. He begins to scan over it, perhaps in hopes of reminding himself why you're there.

"You do read our magazine?" the editor asks without looking up from the resume.

"It's not something I do on purpose," you say.

"It's okay. We can't expect everybody to be a fan. Can we?"

You almost answer his question. Instead you say, "It's not that I'm not a fan." You take a deep breath and exhale slowly into the palms of your hands and then rub the bridge of your nose, and in doing so, notice a small stain, marring the calfskin like a liver spot, on the toe of your right shoe.

"You know," says the editor, somehow pulling a copy of the magazine from under the table, as if it had been resting on his lap during the entire interview. He brandishes it in front of you. "Since you're here, it's probably a good time for me to tell you.

I *can* offer you a discount rate."

"A discount?"

"Yes, a full year, all forty seven issues at a discount. It's a special, professional rate. Something we offer to other members of the media."

"A subscription?"

"Yes. Just talk to the secretary on your way out," says the editor, pounding his fist down on the conference table as he stands up. "Well, I'd say this interview is postponed."

"Until when?" you ask.

"Indefinitely. Just talk to the secretary on your way out. She'll take care of everything. Give her this."

The editor pulls from his pocket what looks like a stack of business cards and hands one card to you. Still sitting in the chair, you look at the card.

1-year subscription to The New Yorker for $20.

There's no reason why the secretary should have to end her phone call, so she continues talking into her headset. You're perfectly fine waiting in silence as she finishes running your Visa through the credit card machine that rests on her desk, actually you're pleasantly surprised that The New Yorker accepts credit cards in the office and you sign the receipt with a satisfying sense of closure.

In the elevator, you reach for the brass button imprinted with L. But then you pause for a second and look above the elevator doors at the small backlit signs designating the floors for other publications housed in the building. Each glows like a small marquee advertising a blockbuster you haven't seen.

SHE HAS THE ROOM ABOVE HIM AND HE HAS THE ROOM NEXT TO HER

Kyle, this malihini from the mainland, wakes up mid-dream with his sweaty head hanging pale over the side of his bed. He thinks for a moment, terrified, that he's still looking at those wawaes. The younger sister, Mele, stomps with the same feet through Kyle's bedroom. She calls out to him that there's a beach; she's going to the beach because it's early and sleeping is too hard, and then she opens the curtains. Mele always leaves the room with the curtains still swinging.

Kyle turns and moans into his pillow.

"Ke kahakai! The beach!" Mele says.

"The what?"

"The beach is a very real place, Kyle. Now wake up!"

When Kyle tries to retreat back under his sheets, Mele likes to scream "Kyyyyllllllllle," with an operatic shrill as she stomps to the kitchen then stirs her single serving of Nescafé. This is Mele's morning routine: being loud, she stirs her coffee, making clings against one of the many mugs she stole from Denny's then she slams the microwave door a couple times in the process of reheating some rice pudding she made earlier in the week. And because she misses her sister, the one who had a mean spike, Mele sets her volleyball to herself and kills it against Kyle's white-painted cinderblock walls until she's dripping sweat and her hand throbs with the pain of the hits. Bam—thunk. Bam—thunk. Bam—thunk.

Kyle's eyes tear up as they adjust to the sunrise that aches its way through his bedroom's salt-crusted window. He tries to explain that he doesn't feel well enough to get up. He had stayed out late and drank on a local's discount at the Honuz

Bar. "Sorry about that, Mele." But Kalani, this am-surfer that tends the bar, can serve a mean White Russian, and that's a hard thing for Kyle to say no to. Really though, Kalani suffers Kyle's indulgence more because he's into Mele and her buxom okole, but Kalani's afraid of the way she bosses him around without even paying attention to him, so all Kalani can do is serve Kyle drinks and hope it brings him closer to Mele; which, it won't because Mele hates it when Kyle stays out drinking and she knows Kalani is the one doling out the drinks. Whenever Kalani serves Kyle his fifth drink Kalani will mention Mele's buxom okole, which bothers Kyle. But the malihini can't figure out if it's because he's being protective like a brother might be or if he's jealous.

"Why do you do this to yourself?" Mele yells from the bathroom. The toilet flushes.

"I'm not doing this to myself. I'm doing this with myself," Kyle says.

"That doesn't mean anything. It sounds cute, but it means absolutely nothing."

Mele comes back into his room, holding her volleyball and wearing her sister's green practice shorts from UH. She flexes angry thighs that would make a masseuse cry. Her sun-streaked black hair, stiff and wavy with yesterday's sand and salt, reaches down to her elbows. Kyle rubs his eyes.

"I don't like it when you look at me that way," she says.

"I wasn't looking at you in any way. I was just looking at you," Kyle says.

But this malihini was admiring her thighs, so Mele hurls the volleyball right by his head and against the wall, causing Kyle to cover up. She snatches the ball as it bounces back. "So can I borrow your board since you're obviously not going anywhere?"

"Yeah, but I haven't patched up that ding," Kyle says.

"Man, still?"

"Fix it for me."

She stomps off again, but not angry. She just stomps all the time, like not wasting time waiting for Kyle. She has a way to handle things. This is the way Kyle remembers it: Mele had kicked another girl's ass after the girl called net and said something about her being too short to hit, that she should stick with digs and sets. After the beat down Mele walked away, calling the battered girl out on her camel toe. "Who plays with that shit hanging out?" she yelled, strutting down the beach to lay on her towel—where she'd throw little shells at unsuspecting tourists, not going back to the game. After that, a lot of people kept a safe distance, never wanted to let things get too serious with her. All the other players thought the bruised-up girl was just trying to give Mele helpful criticism. Moke, a real big and tough dude from down-the-way Waimanalo, called Mele—the moke. Not only is she a badass at the net like her sister was but she's aware of her good looks too. She's had a lot of boys telling her about her, and they all say the same thing, but she's not into a guy that can only tell her something she already knows.

Mele grabs the board, a sky-blue, 6-foot Town and Country surfboard, and starts for the door. "Well, don't blame me if it doesn't seal before I hit the water with it. I mean, it's your board. Also, you're getting fat. And I mean that as a warning, not a criticism," Mele yells as she walks out the door. But Kyle had broken the most basic leash law: left the leash dangling free from the tail of his board. So when Mele walks out, the leash gets caught in the door as it closes. Mele curses, fumbling with her keys to open the door, calling him a moron. He gets out of bed, but as he nears the door, Mele drops the board on the ground. "Fuck it," she says.

He hesitates to open the door, and when he does Mele is already walking down the street. His board wobbles between the last step and the landing, the nose grinding against the concrete.

He tugs the leash out from under the door. He admits that he's gotten a little heavier around the gut, maybe a little under the chin, but not enough that "fatter" is accurate. Kyle goes back to bed.

At ten he gets up again. He has an appointment with a man named Dr. Ho who wears the same kind of flip-flops as Kyle, which makes it easier for Kyle to feel comfortable enough with Dr. Ho to argue with him. Kyle has been talking to Dr. Ho for a few months, ever since his boss at the Star-Advertiser had convinced him that his job, along with everything else Kyle might consider important in his life, depends on coping with and surviving the death of his girlfriend, Ailani.

She'd been killed in a car accident the previous year. Kyle and Ailani were together for four years. Kyle had come to Ailani a tender-footed haole, a refugee from a flooded city back mainland. Ailani had promised him that he'd never have to go back. And so far, he has not gone back. Whether it's because his grief froze his ability to make decisions or because he wants to stay in Kailua to feel closer to Ailani, Kyle has not gone back.

Mele, Ailani's little sister, moved in with Kyle six months after the accident, saying she was sick of city life in Chicago. She was studying politics at Loyola and playing for their volleyball team. "I hate indoor," she said the day she walked into Kyle's house, throwing her backpack on the floor. "I miss the sand." She bought a blow-up mattress and took over Kyle's office.

A lot of people, everybody actually, think it's a bad idea for Mele to be living with Kyle. Nobody will say it's a bad idea, discussing it makes their friends feel too uncomfortable. But Dr. Ho likes to be a bit more direct about his concerns.

"Are you sure she stomps just like her sister? Or do you just think she stomps like her sister?" Dr. Ho says. He's squinting at his snorkeling mask as he rubs it clean with an old, ripped up t-shirt. Dr. Ho is not a counselor or a psychologist or a therapist. He's a marine biologist and spends a lot of time kicking around the reefs, recording evidence of the decline in ringed rice coral.

"I'm sure of it. Mele stomps just like Ailani used to. And there's nothing wrong with me appreciating that."

"What I'm saying is, maybe indulging in the similarities makes it easier for you to deal with losing Ailani. The problem might be that you allow yourself not to differentiate between them."

"Obviously there are similarities. She's her little sister, same blood, and we're helping each other deal with the death."

"But your relationship with her has turned into a companionship, and that could—this is just a worry I have— lead to the kind of shared habits you had with Ailani. Daily rituals, simple stuff like walks for coffee after you wake up. Or television shows that you always watch together, even little things like that, you could end up doing those things with her little sister."

"What's wrong with us depending on each other?"

Dr. Ho tosses his snorkeling mask into a duffel bag and looks at Kyle. He taps Kyle on the shoulder. "I think you should try to find other people to spend time with."

Last night Kyle had tried to spend time with other people and he thought that meant drinking at Honuz, meeting another girl and going home with her if she wanted him to. Lisa was a photographer on assignment for a real estate magazine, taking pictures of property in and around Kailua. In his desperation to try and connect with another person, Kyle answered Lisa's questions, told her where to eat, and where she'd find the best beachfront property.

Kalani stood by the cash register shaking his head when he heard Kyle mention the Kailua favorite beach --------. "Hey, Kyle. Kulikuli!"

"What?" Kyle said.

"Cool it. Shut that spout of yours," Kalani said slowly.

"I'll be right back," Lisa said, looking at Kalani as she walked to the front of the bar.

Kalani made his way down to Kyle.

"What the fuck, Kyle?" he whispered, handing Kyle another beer.

"I just got carried away. You're right. I'll shut up," Kyle mumbled into the cool lip of the beer.

"Yeah, that'd be smart. You think I like wearing this fucking shirt, pouring drinks for all these people?" He tugged at his faded Hawaiian print shirt. His broad shoulders stressed the seams of the shirt as he leaned forward and got in Kyle's face. "It pays the bills but anymore of it and I'd swim for the Philippines. You gonna let her sell it out."

"Alright, alright," Kyle said.

When Lisa hinted later that it was time to go home together, Kyle insisted they go to her place. He couldn't bring another girl home in front of Mele. Or he wasn't sure if he could. At Lisa's hotel they undressed, but then Lisa stopped when she saw the fresh, pink scar that stretched down the right side of Kyle's chest where his rib had snapped and was forced through his skin at impact. Kyle told her about the truck and the heavy rain.

Lisa was quiet for sometime before she got up and put her clothes back on. Kyle got up too and slipped on his shirt and found his flip-flops.

Mele would probably still be awake if Kyle went home. She'd give him hell for drinking. So he stayed in Lisa's hotel room with the idea that he'd leave once it was late enough for Mele to be asleep.

"I'm going to open this," Kyle said, pulling a bottle of champagne out of the fridge. "Is this on the company account?"

"You opened it before you asked."

Kyle slammed the champagne down and watched the bubbles cascade to the blue carpeting. Lisa waved her hand at Kyle to forget about the mess.

"There's this tiny fish, it's only found off Ustica, it's called the Atargatis," Lisa said. "The males are small, about the size of a matchbox. The females are about the size of a pack of cigarettes. When a male fish sees a female fish, most of the time, he'll flee, swim for his life. But when he sees a female that he likes, and he's sure of it, he'll swim in front of her. He'll float in front of her until he's filled with so much excitement and passion that he suddenly bursts, creating a cloud of insides and, of course, cum. The female, sometimes she swims through it with her eggs hanging from her belly. Sometimes she decides, No, she never liked that guy, and she swims around the cloud like somebody avoiding a pothole in the street. Either way, the male fish never knows if the woman of his dreams, his one and only love, ever loved him back."

Kyle stared blankly at Lisa. "That's it?" he asked. "You know that's a load of shit, right? You just keep that little gem around for people like me?"

Lisa shrugged. "Yeah, yeah. But what I'm saying is that the world can only handle so much good fucking."

Lisa took a long drink of the champagne and walked out to the balcony to smoke a cigarette.

"If you're getting more champagne just bring out the whole bottle. I want some more too," Lisa said without turning around.

But Kyle was leaving. As he headed for the door he saw Lisa's notebook poking out from her shoulder bag. He grabbed her notebook and read the names of the places he had told Lisa about, places where he had hiked and camped with Ailani, places where they'd been allowed some lovemaking, places where they'd been allowed some fucking. Then Kyle finally felt angry, and it felt good to be angry. He tore out the pages where she had scribbled his advice. But "shit, why not?" he then said and took the whole notebook. He walked out the door, and on the walk home he tossed the notebook into a trashcan outside of Long's Drug Store.

When he got home he found Mele looking through some of Ailani's art supplies. "I wanted to draw some designs on your surfboard," she said. But she gave up and sat on the futon with Kyle.

They watched Aqua Teen Hunger Force. Sand still covered Mele's legs, and Kyle whined a little about it getting all over the futon. She laughed, kicking her legs up over him and started shaking all the sand off her legs.

"You're like Meatwad," Mele erupted, laughing so hard she dropped the jar of peanut butter. "Meatwad! Oh my god, you're Meatwad!" She used her arm to wipe the peanut butter from the corners of her mouth then she gave Kyle a hug.

"You smell like the inside of a Cosmopolitan magazine. Gross," Mele said. She got up and went into the bathroom.

"You ever see that girl on the courts anymore? The girl you beat on?" Kyle yelled to her.

"What are you talking about? I didn't beat on any girl." She turned on the shower.

"Yeah, she said you couldn't hit and then you kicked her ass and yelled something about camel toe and shit."

"You're crazy, Kyle. That was Ailani that did the ass kicking, like last year. Jeez, man, just watch your television and leave me alone for a bit."

"You're right. Sorry, I'm not sure what I was thinking. I haven't been getting enough sleep."

She came out of the bathroom, walking by with her bath towel on, and went in her bedroom, shutting the door behind her slowly.

"She does a lot of things differently," Kyle says.

"Of course," Dr. Ho says. He's cleaning the straps and buckles on his fins with a different old t-shirt and a little bit of lubricant. He explains that the lubricant keeps the rubber straps from drying and cracking.

"Ailani had some pretty strange habits. She was so earthy she would save her used dental floss, and I would complain about it when I'd walk in the bathroom and see it dangling on the edge of the sink. And now I find myself doing it."

"You've adopted some of her behaviors. That's okay though. It may be a better way to feel closer to her instead of always being with her sister. All I know is that when I tell you to hang out with other people I don't mean you should be trying to get in some stranger's arms. You've got to figure out some stuff by yourself."

For Mele and Kyle, after the first initial flood of sympathy, a change occurred where the friends they loved didn't recognize them anymore, and with enough time might have even mistaken them for strangers on the street. They felt like their old friends didn't know them anymore because of the amputees they'd become, and that new people in their lives could never be their friends because they never knew Ailani. So Kyle and

Mele withdrew into themselves and each other.

Sometimes it felt temporary. Kyle had bought all new linens. But he kept the old ones, folding them neatly and putting them in airtight storage bags he bought at Wal-Mart. He did the same thing with all of Ailani's clothes, as if he was just preparing for a seasonal change. When he wakes up in the morning, lint from the new fabrics is all over his body, clumps of sweaty cotton in the pockets of his knees. His bath towels are new too. When he gets out of the shower and dries off, he has to pick the lint from his body all over again.

Kyle and Ailani had the same-size feet so they shared six different pairs of slippas, all Locals brand purchased for four dollars a pair at Long's Drug Store. Then they were just Kyle's slippas. When Mele moved in with more of the same-size feet she brought two more pairs of the same-size slippas. Now there are eight.

After returning home from his appointment with Dr. Ho, Kyle puts on his board shorts, then picks one blue slippa and one white slippa from the pile, slips his board under his right arm, and goes to catch a bus to the beach and meet up with Mele. He gets on the 70 which takes him down to the park, from there Kyle can walk down to the nets and stumble on Mele playing volleyball or resting between games.

Mele's lying on her towel, sunning, and setting her volleyball to herself. She can lay still, her head and back flat against the ground, setting the ball up against the wind at the perfect angle so that it's blown back to her fingertips where she sets it again. She hardly has to move. Kyle used to watch Ailani and Mele lie next to each other, setting the ball back and forth to each other. Kyle would allow himself to be hypnotized, watching them set to each other like that for twenty minutes at a time, so effortlessly, while they tanned.

Kyle is not that coordinated. He feels goofy and a bit dizzy just walking through the deep, dry sand, his slippas kicking sand against his calves. He flings his slippas off and sits down next to Mele.

"You made it," she says, continuing to set the ball to herself.

"Tide is super low, but the waves are clean," says Kyle.

"Yeah, you should seal that ding and take the board out."

Mele crosses her legs under herself and stands up. She walks to one of the courts, throwing her ball by the back line. Then she wipes the sand off and joins a game.

Kyle rolls on his side and looks through Mele's backpack for the Sun Cure. He grabs it and squeezes the gooey fiber on the hole in the surfboard. Then he smoothes it down with a plumeria leaf he finds in the sand. When he's finished he angles the board at the sun so the fiber can dry.

Mele's yelling, calling hits, calling sets, celebrating kills until her voice goes hoarse.

THREE

TWO MOMENTS WITH THE COMMON SEMI-LATENT PSYCHO

I

Last week I found out Dad keeps the surgical gloves from every cosmetic surgery he performs on Alec Baldwin. I imagine there's a law against it. Or that dad's at least in danger of losing his license. Also, I'm under the assumption that Alec doesn't want anybody knowing he gets work done at all, let alone regularly enough to sustain some sort of museum of surgical artifacts.

How I found the gloves is another story. What happened was mom locked the wireless Internet because she caught me looking at porn. Now the only computer with Internet has a password, and I can only use it when mom or dad is around. After I talked to my friends, mostly dudes but Kelly too, my impression is that I wasn't doing anything nobody else is doing.

At least I'm not collecting bloody gloves and endangering the wellbeing of my entire family. Anyway, I found the gloves while looking to see if dad still had some Hustlers I'd found back when I was in middle school.

I was digging through dad's walk-in closet when I started sneezing. I would realize later when Kelly and I tried to have sex for the first time that I have a latex allergy. But there they were, each pair labeled with Alec Baldwin and a date, in a big box frame like one of those butterfly collections.

So I took my weirdo dad's collection of squeaky, green gloves covered in the blood of Alec Baldwin and hid them in my room, which is gross, but worth it. I'm going to let dad squirm for a while and then I'll make a deal with him for the

Internet. Kelly said I need to think bigger, "like Alec Baldwin bigger," she said. Then she stopped answering my texts.

II

Our landlord said he would do some renovations while we were out of town visiting Kelly's parents. "Modernize the whole place," he said. "It'll be better. Trust me."

At first, with its open floor plan, tall ceilings, hardwood floors, and rustic cabinetry, it seemed way sexier than our old wall-to-wall carpeted one bedroom. Way more feng shui or whatever.

Sexy was important because we liked things that kept us fucking. The old apartment was not keeping us fucking. The wall-to-wall carpeting made clean up a nightmare.

But after a week of great sex, we realized that because there were no doors, not even for the bathroom, we couldn't install peepholes.

I'll explain: we liked peepholes because we liked watching one another. In our old apartment I'd installed peepholes in every door. We could watch one another pee, cook, eat, bathe, or feign sleep. All of this involved masturbation in some way, on both ends.

But this loss of peepholes made our entire sex life unravel into a monotony we'd never experienced before. We would just pee to pee, or bathe to bathe, or cook to cook…you get the point.

One day I came home with a bag full of peepholes I got at the Ace and told Kelly to glue them to my glasses.

She protested, "We can find new things! You have to be more adventurous than this, for us."

I yelled at her that this would work and that everything would go back to normal.

"Maybe normal is no longer enough," she said, as she gently

applied the peepholes to my lens. When she finished she asked, "What should *I* do?"

Kelly doesn't have glasses. I looked at her, and then I started getting turned on. I didn't want it to happen right away, but it did. So I told her, "Leave me."

She walked out the door, touching herself the entire time. And that was the sexiest time a woman has ever left me.

BELATONE ISLAND HAS SEVEN RESIDENTS: OUR MAWS AND PAWS, YOU, ME, AND MICRO

Maw 2 and Paw 2 order us to find wood without grit in its veins ("It's a matter of survival"). We ignore the order and focus on the moat we're building around Fortress 1, our fortress, that's been the thing ever since the Maws and Paws started letting us sleep together. To us, it's most important that we build fortress 1's moat before we invest too much time into building the actual fortress. All we got is a bed under a tin roof that shakes and thunders atop four logs. But we'll do more after we have the moat. You've got to be all about insuring things when you live on Belatone Island.

I get hit on the head twice by one coconut: the first time when it falls from its tree, the second time when you throw it at me because I try to bury my face in your pussy.

We're supposed to be working, you say. You tell me to keep digging; I'm thirsty and there's a ringing inside my head for you. You shovel some sand into your panties ("For later"). You know I like sand on your toes and a little in my mouth.

You explain, Not that I don't want your mouth on me, but Paw 1 will kill you. We shan't take advantage of the numbnut's generosity in letting us two sleep together.

The Maws and Paws have accepted certain things if they let us sleep together, is my argument.

We're thirteen. They expect us to act thirteen, you say.

I stare at the sides of you that come out around the trim of your panties. You see me lost for a moment and you like it, letting your legs remain open, your sometimes veiled crotch touching the wet sand of our beach. You continue to dig our moat.

Then, with the break of a small wave, some drowned furry animal of a thing washes up on our beach. It's a dog. It's a dog with no hind legs. By that I mean it's a quadruped that only has front paws. It drags itself up the beach, closer to us, before letting out a little yelp, then a huff, as it collapses.

You say, We have to help it.

I say, I know.

You say, We'll call it Micro.

Micro helps dig the moat because the dog only has two front legs and it digs, pretty much automatically, anywhere you lay the poor thing, like it's still dog paddling for its life out there in the ocean. Micro has sad eyes that say, Listen I know I only have two front legs and you have to pretty much carry me everywhere but at least I can do this and I will for as long as I can muster.

You say, It makes me kind of sad.

I say, Me too, but I feel like it might be unfair to tell him, or her, to stop.

Yes, you say, we all need our reason to live.

We lay Micro where we want our foundation and Micro digs it.

TAKE YOUR BOOTS OFF BEFORE THE STORM

It hadn't been on course for us, but when Rem got excited, I got excited, and then it hit. That was, and has been, the course of events. Rem, of green eyes that calm seizures, has pooled my river. I sensed things but didn't know urgency like Rem. The best way to explain was together; ever since the night she yelled my name. I'm still not sure how she'd known my name. "You know me," she'd said.

So I believed her and moved in with her and then the storm came. She bought batteries. I bought beer. She bought candles. I bought saltines. When branches blew through our windows and waves crested the porch, even snakes swam to us for help and we gave it to them in what tupperware we still had; I saw a squirrel give up and swirl under for good, its black eyes gazing up to admire the rush of clouds one last time. We went inside, up to our bedroom, and barricaded the door with piles of unbounded books. We cradled one another and entwined; I lost mixtapes of hours then days, and she made hit records on a juice harp stuck inside of me. But I could feel something at work on me and in me: a stitching, massaging, gluing, and sometimes it almost hurt but most of the time it felt good and it felt like her, but, like I said, I'm not sure what I'm remembering right.

Then there was no more to be done, so when I came to, and saw her eyes again, those green eyes, waiting, I got up with her and we walked outside and even picking plastic grocery bags out of our tree was the best thing in the world.

TUXEDO LIFE

There is a bird I don't know monkeying crows. It flies from one tree to far neighbor. It has color but all I see is black. There is a car hovering on wheels above guttered water, eyes that neither one of us saw but I said. When I touch you I apologize for nothing. But it sticks like yellow snow by my empty mailbox.

How many times is too many I love yous. One and then two. Many times. I had arugula on my lip but I swear I still felt your sexy. I sogged the bread with balsamic but you still said it was good. Mom said Love to y'all. But then she had to see Nobi about her hair and said goodbye.

When I'm on our porch and you're on your way home I'm not talking on the phone, stretching my legs, or smoking a cigarette. Why it takes so long to make a left turn here, or parallel park a compact car.

If we met Beyoncé would we take a picture with her? Would there be time to choose a filter? And who would have been adequately insured to rent me a tux. You could use my cummerbund as a night mask. What a "Word!" you used.

THE KOALA CONCEPTION

When Reb told me we were having a koala I just kissed her cheek, sort of smiled like a dickhead, and thought to myself, that's so cute she's already giving our baby little pet names.

Then she showed me what was an extremely detailed ultrasound. I didn't know they could be so detailed. And it *was* a koala. Just like what you learned about as a kid or saw in the zoo. The thing you see eating eucalyptus leaves. The whole Australian, koala critter.

"A koala bear? How?" I asked her.

"It's actually just *koala*. It's not a bear. It's a marsupial," she said.

"Okay. But still," I said.

"What that means is the baby will be here in about 15 days, because, you know, koalas only have a gestation of 35 days tops, which means we need to construct some kind of pouch for me to wear so it can finish developing, which then takes another four months or so," she said, bustling her baggy flannel shirt into a pouch for emphasis, I guessed.

"This is a lot to take in, love. I'm still wondering why we're having a koala bear. I mean, koala."

"Listen, everybody is just as nervous as you. Dr. Andrews just said we have to take it one day at a time."

"But that's what she said when we *found out* you were pregnant!" I argued.

"Mitch, there's just no time to stand here wondering how it all happened or how it's gonna happen. It's happening! I have to go figure out this pouch thing. I'm thinking of fashioning this into some sort of satchel," she said, bending over and grabbing a pink UGG boot from under our bed. "I can't believe

Aunt Nettle thought I'd wear these."

Although she would kill me for using the term fem-punk, Reb is in a fem-punk band called The Crags. Her musical and fashion sense is like Hole meets Patti Smith meets Stevie Nicks, so the pink UGG boots were never of much use to her.

"Yet, here we are. Man, I'm feeling a little overwhelmed," I said.

She walked over to me and pressed her forehead against my lips. "Me too. Let's try to relax. Go teach. Life goes on, love. Bills have to be paid. Eucalyptus leaves are more expensive than you'd think."

"Really?"

"Yeah, Euc Products of California. You can order online, like $20 a pound."

"Right," I said.

"Plus shipping," she said, jabbing a steak knife through the UGG boot. "Can you stop at Ace and see if they have some leather rope on your way home?"

"Sure," I mumbled. "Love you."

"Thanks. I love you."

I tried to teach as usual. It was our day to cover Pi; in fact, it was Pi Day. I like to think the kids get a kick out of talking Pi theory on March 14th, but in all likelihood they're bored with it. It was, after all, a common curriculum course and they've probably been bored with Pi since the sixth grade. Anyway, I couldn't concentrate.

My lecture came to a stuttering halt and I stared down at my leather Chacos with a complete loss for words. Then, suddenly I blurted out, "What are the chances of a human birthing a koala?"

"Pi over zero!" Keith answered, which was followed by a

little chorus of laughter.

Keith's a bit of a prick. Every class has one. They tend to be males. But Keith's an exception because despite being a prick I like him. I like him because he pays attention, he doesn't text in class, and while his comments can be a little knee jerkish or brash, at least he's participating. His attendance is a little sketchy, but I know it's because he's juggling a part time job at Wal Mart; I saw him gathering shopping carts once when I was on an errand for a space heater. He's always wearing khakis and a white polo shirt, which I'm assuming is most of his uniform. He's got a hellish bus commute from N.O. East too. He's probably in his mid-20s; a young black man in N.O. East doesn't have it easy.

"Pi over zero, Professor Mitch?" he said, feigning seriousness this time.

"You're wrong, Keith. So wrong," I said, still staring down at my Chacos; my shoulders slumped over. I felt tears welling up and I rubbed my eyes. "I don't know what the chances are exactly. But I know it's not zero, Keith."

I grabbed my bag and left. I didn't even erase the board, which is something I usually take pride in doing out of consideration for other adjuncts.

By the time I got to Ace, my rateyourprofessor page already had three new entries. Ugly entries. Words like "super weird," "insecure," "not bad looking, but not stable." I'd taken to checking it as a nervous habit because I was under some impression that it affected my chances of getting hired full-time, which, since we were having a koala, would really help with insurance. It wasn't that I was ungrateful for the adjunct gigs; I liked working with the students, but there's this weird duality: the privilege of even having the advance degree that makes you qualified for an adjunct gig at a community college, which then pays you so little, which makes it a fucking privilege to be so broke. But I'm thirty with a baby on the way now, so living paycheck to paycheck and not having insurance is pretty worrisome.

I went inside Ace and found some leather rope in the crafts section. On my way to the register I saw a huge box with a big picture of a treehouse on it. "The Complete Tree House Kit," it said, with a picture of a dad smiling up at what I assumed were his son and daughter waving and laughing with their human hands and mouths. "The One and Only Complete Kit," it said in smaller print.

It was $300. If I got it our electric bill would have to be late again.

"Any kid would love this, right?" An Ace employee stood next to me, nodding his head up and down. He had big grey, bushy sideburns. "If they'd had this when I was a kid, it sure would've saved my dad a huge headache. You got a tree climber back at home?" he asked.

"A tree climber?" I said. His nametag read Tom. "Yes. Yeah, I have a kid."

"Great. I bet your kid will love this."

"I'm the one that'll need a tree house. It, I mean, my baby'll be right at home in the trees, Tom," I said, gazing at the kit, considering what tools I'll need.

I looked up from the kit and Tom was staring at me a bit confused, but mostly sympathetic, I thought.

Tom, bushy sideburns fluttering in the wind, helped me tie the box to the top of my Kia.

The parking on our block was all taken, so I double-parked to unload the tree house. As I put the car in park, the engine light came on. That was when I decided that the electric bill would have to come before the Kia.

When I came through the front door dragging the box, Reb was standing in front of our cracked bedroom mirror, her tank top pulled up, exposing her tummy, which now, already, showed a curve up toward her breasts. Her skin glowed golden in the paper lamplight as she rubbed cocoa butter on the new bump. I stopped at the sight of her. I was grateful.

She was holding the UGG boot, now refashioned into a satchel, against her chest. "Did you get the rope?" she asked.

"Yes," I said.

In its torn and repurposed state, the UGG boot now looked punk, if not at least alternative verging on punk.

"What's that giant thing?" she asked, nodding at the box next to me.

"Our tree house, I guess."

"Perfect," she said. I dragged the box into the living room, I walked into the bedroom, and Reb and I made love.

Any other night I probably would've fallen right into a deep, safe sleep, but that night, I stared at the alarm clock counting down to the moment when Reb would realize she could do, scratch that, *deserved* way better than me. Reb, of body changing and way more invested in it all than me, has the right to ask for and get whatever she wants. And what shall I, doofus donning Chacos, provide? The thing is, I knew she wasn't expecting anything from anyone because she'd always been just fine on her own.

Reb slept weird. I watched her tummy rise and fall with her breathing all night. Whatever was in there kicked two times at 3:12am. Her poor tummy distended in all sorts of directions, enough so that you'd freak. Any normal, caring person would freak.

In a panic, thinking that something needed to be done, I got up and grabbed a fresh roll of paper towels and laid them out all around Reb's thighs and legs. After that, nothing happened. She farted a little and then mumbled, "Sorry, bubs."

I sipped on a Big Shot to pass the time.

The next morning, after the restless night, I made a mistake and drank 36 ounces of coffee before and during my lecture. My energy infected class discussion, and I provoked some note taking and a few chuckles, but the whole thing felt a little unfocused.

"Professor Mitch, is it fair to say that the study of infinite numbers won't prepare me to be a CPA?" Claire asked.

"Anything's possible, Claire, right?" I said.

"Not if you're a boring ass CPA!" Keith said.

"Keith, that's a little unfair and a little too easy, don't you think?" I said.

"I was just backing you up, professor," Keith said.

I was debating whether or not I should explain that my father was a CPA and a fun guy to be around, but then I noticed time was up and called class. I was happy to retreat to the bathroom.

I settled in the third stall and pulled my phone out to read the news and distract myself from concerns of my lectural inadequacies. Oddly enough, that day, the news feeds were quiet, not a shooting or a bombing or a decree or a fatwah or murder-suicide or a consumer stampede to be Googled, the kind of rare day that makes you feel confident bringing new life into the world.

Then the bathroom door opened. I saw some khaki pants and black All Stars shuffling across the tiled floor, by my stall, and over to a urinal. Right as it seemed the All Star might commence to peeing, he turned and approached my third stall.

"Professor Mitch! Is that you?"

The voice was recognizable.

"Keith?"

"Professor Mitch, I knew it was you! I'd recognize those sandals anywhere!"

The All Stars shuffled a bit closer toward my stall door, and I instinctually hugged my bag against my chest. Then I dropped my damn phone. It bounced off my big toe, which ended up hurting a lot more than you'd think, landing finally on the tile floor right beyond the stall door. I froze, being really unsure of what to do next.

"I got it!" Keith said, and before I could say anything he had scooped the phone up and was holding it under the stall door for me to grab.

I didn't take it right away. I guess I was a little surprised, sitting there, pants still down around my ankles and all. So Keith then got down on a knee, stretching his arm out and up even more so the phone was pretty much touching my knees.

"Can you reach it now?" he said.

I grabbed the phone. "Thanks, Keith."

"Professor Mitch, no offense, but you need an upgrade," he said.

"What?" Honest, I wasn't sure what he was talking about at first.

"Your phone. That thing is like four years old." He was standing now.

"Yeah, it's on the list, Keith. Right behind the electric bill and the Kia."

"Whatever you say, Professor Mitch. Anyway, I wanted to talk to you more about what you were saying the other day. About the chances of a human having a koala baby or something. I think I know what you were getting at."

"Can we do this during office hours or just any other time?" I said.

"How about before class, so I don't have to take off work?"

"Perfect," I said. "Come at about 10 or so. I'd appreciate it. And thanks for helping me out with the phone."

"Cool. Okay, well, I see you then."

The All Stars started heading toward the door. I was wondering if he forgot to pee. Then Keith stopped and said, "I just want to say, Professor Mitch, that I think you're a cool guy."

I didn't say anything.

"What I mean is, I like your style," he said finally.

I knew I had to say something. And as I sat there, struggling to find some polite reply to send him on his way so I could pull up my pants, I realized he wasn't talking about my teaching or me as some professor. He was just talking about the regular old day-to-day Big Shot sipping, delinquent bill paying me. "That's nice of you to say, Keith. I think you're a cool guy too. After this I feel like we're practically family, sort of," I said.

"See you Thursday at 10," he said and walked out the door.

That night, after grading some multiple choice quizzes, I headed to Checkpoint Charlie's to catch the end of a Crags show. When I walked in they were doing what really was a sexy (sultry?) cover of Weezer's "Undone," and I got a little choked up because Reb always makes fun of me for loving that song. I play it when I do the dishes. "What a dork!" she'd say, grabbing a towel to help dry, or just smacking me on the ass on her way to the backyard, where I like to think she would dance to the song in secret.

Anyway, I was touched. And then, just as the song was quieting at the end of the climax, a girl sitting at a table by the stage blew some cigarette smoke that happened to go right into Reb's face. It was an accident; the girl was in mid conversation not really paying attention. But suddenly Reb, barefooted, which I hadn't noticed until then, kicked the table over and sent the girl and her friends sprawling to the ground. Reb turned to her band and shrugged her shoulders, then she grabbed the mic. "I know this is a smoker's bar, but the next cunt that blows smoke in my face is getting this Jazzmaster right up the ass!"

The girl and her friends picked their phones up, gave Reb the bird, and left.

"Encore!" I yelled, but it came out sounding more like a question. The Crags huddled around the kick drum to recover, I guessed.

I snuck a shot of Herradura and cringed a little as they tried to win the audience back, but it was too slow of a night for people to forget. I helped them pack up.

We were standing on the empty stage; Reb was still barefoot, which made me nervous.

"Where are your shoes?" I said.

"Over there," she said, pointing at her Luccheses sitting in a little heap behind the stage. "My feet were too swollen. I had to take them off."

"Geez, I'm sorry." I felt directly responsible.

"I feel bad about yelling at that girl. It just came out of me," Reb said. "I didn't even think about it. Should I feel bad?"

"Hell no," I said. "And anybody that knows you knows you'd never do anything that might hurt your Jazzmaster. Did you ride your bike?"

"No, I got nervous about riding and took the bus instead." Reb put her arms around my shoulders and let her body hang. "This feels good on my back."

"Take your time," I said.

I looked down and noticed she was starting to sprout some little zits on her shoulders. "These are cute," I said, scratching at one.

"I'm gross!"

"I don't think so," I said, holding her from pulling away.

"Well, good. Cause everything I read says it's only going to get worse."

Keith didn't show up to our meeting Thursday, and he didn't come to class either. At first I didn't give it a thought. Actually, I was kind of a dick about it, assuming he was being flaky like the other students, which is shitty thinking in general, and a line of thought I find myself fighting pretty regularly. Then he didn't come to class at all the next week, so I emailed him. This kind of thing happens a lot, but I was worried and kept emailing him because he'd expressed such an interest in the class, sort of an interest in the class, maybe more of an interest in my life, so yeah, I guess my concern for him was mostly rooted in his initial concern for me. He wasn't responding to my emails.

Reb and I went in for her final appointment with Dr. Andrews. The baby was due in three days. The technician wouldn't say anything; I don't think they're allowed to. But the baby had developed enough that, when we were watching the ultrasound, it was even more obvious that it was a koala. I don't know what I was expecting—some sort of miraculous switcheroo in the womb?

Dr. Andrews didn't say much. "Everything looks great! Let's have a baby!" That was it, really.

We went home really happy. Reb was smiling and slapping her hands on her thighs the whole ride home, singing, "We're gonna have a baby! We're gonna have a baby!" I was honking the Kia horn as we spiraled down the hospital's parking deck exit ramp. Still, that damn engine light was glowing red in my face the whole ride home.

Then, we sat on the porch and took in the night air. A cool front had moved all the humidity out. On nights like these we would normally drink wine until we couldn't see straight, or Reb couldn't play the acoustic anymore, whichever came first.

She was strumming on her cheap no-name acoustic, the guitar's body resting on the arm of the chair while the neck was just barely touching her tummy. "I'm pretty sure things will never be the same, and I'll miss some stuff, but I'll be happier than I've ever been too. I'm pretty sure," she said.

"Yeah me too. Just some things I still want to do. Just to have everything squared away, so I feel that we're prepared. Although, there's no way to really prepare for it all, I guess.

"You know, you don't have to figure everything out tonight or tomorrow or any other time before the baby. You know that, right? It's called a due date, but it's not a deadline, bubs." She said it sternly. Then she put her guitar down so that she could give me a long, hard kiss, the kind that makes my lips go numb against her imperfect teeth. "You can still be who you are now," she said.

"You too," I said.

Before getting in bed I checked my email, something I like to do to avoid any surprises the next day. Keith had emailed me. He was apologizing for missing the classes and asking if he could meet with me tomorrow. I told him we'd talk after class.

My lecture went a little long that morning, mostly I think because it took me a while to get to the heart of the lesson. Sometimes I like to try and get the students to talk about whatever, get a bead on what the buzz is these days and then move into the lesson; that way we all find ourselves talking about the material without really realizing it. But then my phone chimed, telling me I had a text, and I realized it was almost 11:30.

It was Reb. "Feel like something is pushing against my tailbone."

I responded, "Like pain? Be more specific?"

"Like I have to poop," she said.

"Okay, I have to meet with a student real quick, probably no more than five minutes, and then head home. Let me know if anything changes," I said.

Keith was packing up slowly, waiting for me to finish my texting. He had the same black All Stars, khakis and white polo on as usual; they looked a little beat up now from all the parking lot work, I guessed.

"You mind if we find a bench or picnic table outside, Professor Mitch? I don't want anybody barging in on us."

"Sure, Keith." I was pretty sure he wanted to lay on in dramatic fashion his excuse for being gone in hopes that I'd be cool with all the absences. I'd already decided that I'd just make him do a bunch of equation exercises to make up for it. But I genuinely wanted to hear him out, get an idea of what was going on in his life.

We found a bench by some of the bike racks and sat down. "I had this older cousin," he started immediately, which I kind of liked a lot more than some bullshit questions about how I might be doing to try and soften me up. "This dude was crazy. He was an asshole. Sorry, Professor Mitch, but he was."

"Hey, no worries, Keith. Tell it like it is."

"He lived down the street from me my whole life. Used to beat the shit out of me. Did the same kind of thing to my little sister. When we were really young, he'd make us run errands to other houses in the neighborhood, until we got old enough to know what was going on. Anyway, dude got killed like ten days ago."

"Jesus, Keith. I'm sorry to hear that," I said. I don't know. What else can you say?

"First few days, me and my sister didn't care. You know, the guy was an asshole, like I said. But then suddenly we did care. It's been hard. Makes me think about a lot of bad stuff going on."

"I'm sure. It'd be odd if it didn't." We were sitting there for a minute or so. He wasn't saying anything else. "Listen, Keith. You heading home after this?" I asked.

"No. To work."

"How about I drop you off on my way home?"

"It's on your way?"

"Sort of."

"Alright then. I probably won't be late again that way."

We walked over to the Kia and got in. Keith put his backpack at his feet and pulled out his blue Wal Mart vest. His name was scratched out with the name "K-Rod" Sharpied above it, which I'm assuming is a play on his full name, Keith Rodney.

"I'm surprised they let you get away with doing that to your nametag, the way that place is."

"I know, but I don't plan on being there forever, Professor Mitch," he said.

"Well yeah, I figured that," I said and headed up the I-10 onramp. "What are you going to school for?"

"Welding."

"Good job security I guess, right."

"At least 40K a year, too."

"Shit. Maybe I should become a welder."

"Ha! Professor Mitch. Those dudes on the rigs would eat you alive. No offense."

"Keith, just call me Mitch. I'm not all nerd and sandals over here." I noticed the engine light flickered a bit and then stayed on. "Damn engine light."

"Mitch, you need an upgrade. You need a ride and phone upgrade."

"We aren't all living on a welder's salary."

"I have to ask, Mitch," he said, smiling at me. "Remember all that talk about a koala and a human having a koala or whatever? What was that all about?"

"I was trying to come to terms with the possibility of a human having a koala baby and not a human baby. That's exactly what I was doing. That's it."

"Well, I don't know anything about how possible it is or whatever the hell you're saying, but I'm pretty sure it just doesn't matter. You give birth to something; you love it. Look at my dead cousin, for example. Nasty dude, horrible human being. Even hit his mom once. But for some reason, she's sad, we're all sad he's gone. And koalas are fucking cute. My cousin was no koala."

"Probably not. That's a great way to think about it. It's like this engine light here; it's designed to come on if the smallest thing isn't working perfectly. But that's not how life is!"

"I don't know if that's the same thing, but it sounds good. See that's what I missed about your classes. We just bullshit."

"But it's a good bullshit."

"Yeah. Most of the time."

"Fair enough."

Just then my phone chimed with a text. It was Reb. "Where are you?" she said. I was going to text her but then she called. I answered.

"Are you almost home? We need to go," she said right when I picked up.

"It's happening?" I said. "It's early!"

"It's coming now. My contractions are already two minutes apart, bubs. Come get me!"

I looked over at Keith. He was covering his mouth to hide

his laughter.

"I'll be there in about fifteen minutes. Get in the tub and breathe."

"I'm in the tub now! I thought you were coming home."

"I was dropping a student off on the way," I said this as I was exiting I-10 to turn around. Reb hung up.

"Keith, is there somewhere I can drop you off right now?"

"Just go, Mitch. You'll need all the help you can get," he said, still laughing a bit.

At that point, I just wanted to get home so I kept driving without really thinking about anything else. I drove hard; the Kia made some awful sounds, the kind that remind you that an engine is made of metal, high pitched, gear whining, hot metal. And the smell, like burning plastic.

"What about work?" I said, suddenly remembering what we'd been doing.

"Fuck that job!"

"Yeah, fuck that job," I said a little cautiously.

"I'll have my certification in like two months."

"Right. Welding. You'll do a couple extra assignments to make up for the shit you missed. Everything will be okay." I exited onto Claiborne.

"Yep, everything."

I turned onto my street and skidded to stop on the broken asphalt in front of our house. Unlocking the front door and running straight back to the bathroom, I found Reb sitting naked in the tub squeezing a gym sock in each hand as she fought through each contraction. The water in the tub had a slightly pink and cloudy coloration.

"I don't know if I can stand," she said. "It feels like it's just going to drop right out of me."

"You have to. We have to go. Keep squeezing the socks," I said, grabbing her dress from the floor. I helped her up; her legs were shaky. I helped her slip the dress over her head and walked her to our bedroom. I lifted her onto our bed.

Keith poked his head through the front door and looked around before walking inside. "Can I help with anything?"

"See that weird pink boot thing? Grab that. Meet us in the car. Do you mind driving?"

"Yeah, I'll drive. What was this, an UGG or something?" he said, peering into the furry vacancy.

I ran back to our kitchen and grabbed a bottle of lemonade. I brought it back to Reb, opened it up, and put it to her lips. "Remember? You need the calories, love?"

She took a little sip and then stopped. "I can't. I just don't want it."

"Just one big sip. Please."

She did it, and I helped her stand again. We walked out to the Kia, and Keith was waiting in the driver's seat with the car running.

We headed back towards Claiborne. Reb was breathing really hard, almost hyperventilating; she was working through contractions, which were now right on top of each other. "Oh my God, this really sucks," she said between breaths. I was having a hard time getting her to make eye contact with me.

We turned onto Claiborne, and just when it seemed like everything was going to be okay, that we would make it to the hospital, the Kia started coughing smoke out from under its hood. "Keep going, Keith. Fuck this car, just keep going," I said. Then, a clacking noise started, and it got louder and faster each time Keith accelerated.

"Oh man, that's no good, y'all," Keith said.

And then the clacking and the engine just stopped. We coasted for about 200 feet or so in what was a very weird silence.

Keith pulled over to the side of the road. "I'm going to take a look. Y'all sit tight." After searching a second for the hood release, he popped it and got out.

I rubbed Reb's lower back. She started crying a little.

"Push harder," she breathed. "Against my tailbone."

I adjusted myself so I could apply more pressure. "

It's gonna happen here!" Reb yelled.

"I think it threw a rod! Engine's seized up," Keith said. "I'm calling 911."

"It's happening now!" Reb yelled.

Things got so frantic from that point. I'm not sure of everything that was said or of everything that I saw and Keith saw and Reb saw.

What I do remember, is that in some kind of awesome display of instinct, Reb spun around and threw a leg over my head, grabbing her knees and opening her legs wide. That was when I saw the head. For some reason, all I could do was laugh. This fuzzy head getting squeezed to all hell. With each contraction, Reb would bear down, her face swelling, red, pushing so hard it looked like her head would pop. And the baby's head would pulse out, and then at the end of each contraction, retract back in a little. It was agonizing and completely awe-inspiring.

I told Keith to give me the UGG. I wedged it between my knees so that the opening was positioned for me to place the baby in it immediately. Reb pushed harder and harder; each time, I thought there's no way she could push harder than that, and then she would push even harder and even longer. I looked up and saw Keith with his hands cupped over his mouth.

"Come on, baby. Come on, baby," Reb yelled; I'm sure of that. She kept saying that, like she was cheering the baby on. She sucked in her lips and leaned her head forward, taking in a deep breath. I pushed against her knees. Reb let out what was a really cute grunt and then just yelled, one long sustained yell, nothing like I'd even ever heard at her Crags shows. She yelled and yelled, and then suddenly, like an above ground pool spilling over and collapsing, the baby came sliding out on a river of hot water and blood and the smell was like warm, wet soil. I caught the baby and put it in the UGG and immediately brought it up to Reb's chest. We were doing and saying everything you'd expect us to; we were crying, laughing, saying, Oh My God, Baby, and I clearly remember Keith then saying, "See? I told you so, Mitch. Y'all love it."

ACKNOWLEDGMENTS

Without the support of the following, this book would not be possible.

My teachers: Dr. Mary McCay, Christopher Chambers, Key Randolph, Ron Smith, Brian Morton, Darin Strauss, Breyten Breytenbach, Yusef Komunyakaa, E.L. Doctorow, David Lipsky, and Ralph Adamo.

The editors and publishers of the publications in which a lot of this material originally appeared: *Banango Street, Chicago Quarterly Review, Xavier Review, Everywhere Stories, Otis Nebula, Big Muddy, The Rogue Voice, The Tishman Review,* and *Fiction Southeast.*

My students: Especially Rose Dicks, Nelle Edge, Joe Gehringer, and Anna Schulte, for your sharp reads.

My friends and family: Vincent Cellucci for being my backup breather. Hiram Mechling for putting a roof over my head those eight months after grad school. Benito Segovia for the design work and for innumerable post-Katrina mornings watching cable TV in our boxers and finishing handles of rum. Chef SGT Michael Thibodeaux, Chef Charles Vincent and Chef Garrett Lennon for the nourishment. Jesse Phillips for a soundtrack. Ayesha Attah, Anissa Bazari, Kate Brittain, Anelise Chen, Jan Edwards, Grant Ginder, Sasha Graybosch, MK Hall, Grant Munroe, Max Ross, Brian Trimboli, and Sarah Willeman for the line edits. Dr. Brian Payne for the free diagnoses. Bobby, DD, and Jeff Mitchell. Charles and Charlotte Nabholz. Sarah Mitchell. My grandparents, Fred and Peg Weidman, and Mel and Louise Burgess. Maureen, Susan, and Laura Beamer for showing me how to keep going. Sharon Anderson for always checking up on me. Desha.

My parents and their unwavering patience and encouragement.

My wife, Ryan, and the strength and inspiration she provides every day.

32845846R00090

Made in the USA
Middletown, DE
20 June 2016